THE HAUNTED PRAM:

And Other True New England Ghost Stories

by

Edward Lodi

Rock Village Publishing
41 Walnut Street
Middleborough MA 02346
(508) 946-4738

THE HAUNTED PRAM:

And Other True New England Ghost Stories

by

Edward Lodi

Rock Village Publishing
Middleborough, Massachusetts

First Printing

DEDICATION

To Ric and Yoko
and, of course, Winslow

Acknowledgments

The chapters titled "The Haunted Pram," "The 1725 Captain Taylor House," "The Woman in the White Dress," "The Black Dog of North Carver," and "Tales of Two Witches" originally appeared (in somewhat different form) in the chapbook, *Ghosts in Black and White: Some Hauntings in Plymouth County*, published by Rock Village Publishing in 2001.

Some of the material included in "From the Archives" is in the public domain and is duly credited in that section.

This collection, frankly, is for those who want to be given a bit of a turn, who want to experience that frightening feeling of cosmic insecurity, those who might know what it is like to come for a moment face to face with something immeasurably terrifying. . . .
August Derleth, Sleep No More

The stories that make up the contents of *The Haunted Pram* fall roughly into two categories: accounts of true hauntings which have been related to the author and researched by him; and tales, for the most part obscure, which he found in old books and which he has adapted, embellished, and annotated.

Contents

THE HAUNTED PRAM
(Plymouth, Massachusetts)

And so, it is said, you are haunted!
My friend, we are haunted all;
And every homestead holds a ghost
That ever has held a pall.

Do you think that the empty cradle
Has never a ghost within?
Or the unused nursery table
Hears never a ghostly din?

Think you there is never a patter
Of unseen feet on the floor?
Or that never a voiceless clamour
Floats in through the garden door?

—from "Haunted!" by Isabella Banks

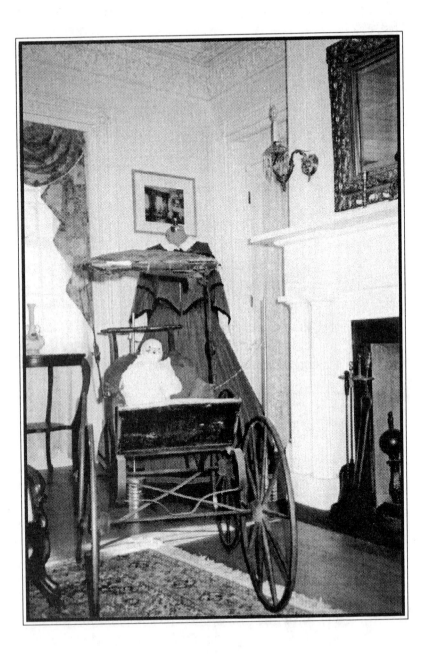

One day while browsing through an antique shop in the town of Kingston, Massachusetts, Ric Cone came upon a perambulator suspended high on a rack in the rear of the shop. The pram, although quite ancient, appeared to be in excellent condition. Why, Ric wondered, was it kept hidden in such an out-of-the-way location? And why, when he questioned the shopkeeper—from whom he'd often purchased items in the past—did the man suddenly seem reluctant to talk?

Ric contemplated buying the pram because he thought it might help preserve the nineteenth-century atmosphere of the Taylor-Trask Museum in Plymouth, of which he is curator and director. In centuries past the fine old building had been the private residence of several prominent families; it was not inconceivable that such a pram had once featured in the daily routine of at least one of the households.

Because he felt it was so appropriate for the museum, he was more than willing to pay the four or five hundred dollars which he knew the perambulator to be worth. Imagine his delight when the shopkeeper quoted a price of less than one hundred dollars!

"Why so cheap?" Ric asked.

"I just want it out of here," the man replied.

Not one to pass up a great bargain, Ric didn't question the man any further but bought the pram and immediately placed it in the historic house on North Street, which he'd only recently established as a museum.

It wasn't long after purchasing the pram that Ric began to have an inkling as to why the shopkeeper had let it go so cheaply: the pram seemed to have a will of its own.

During the night it moved.

In the morning when he opened up the museum Ric often found the pram in a location other than the one in which he'd left it. Sometimes it rested only an inch or two away from its original location; sometimes it had traveled several feet, or even all the way across the room. Whether the pram shifted position by itself, or whether some other agency was involved, Ric couldn't say.

On one occasion when Ric's partner, Yoko, unlocked the museum she found the pram jammed in the doorway, blocking the entrance, as if during the night someone had tried to push it out. More than one visitor to the museum has actually claimed to have seen the pram move, seemingly of its own volition.

For a time, to add period ambiance, Ric kept an antique wax doll—on loan from his gift shop next door—in the perambulator. But regardless of how the doll was placed in the evening, in the morning it always seemed to be gazing out the window.

One day an unsuspecting Yoko unlocked the museum door only to find the pram turned on its side—as if violently tossed there—with the wax doll lying face down. After that episode Ric decided to sell the troublesome doll. He was only too happy to donate to the museum the three hundred dollars he received for it at auction.

Meanwhile the perambulator continues to live up to its name (derived from the Latin *per*, meaning "through," and *ambulare*, "to walk"). The pram "walks" at night. Or perhaps, more accurately, it is pushed. For one evening at a seance held at the Taylor-Trask Museum a noted psychic offered an explanation for the pram's odd behavior.

It is caused, she said, by a little boy from the eighteenth century who wore wooden braces and was unable to move around and play with other children, and who died young. It is his restless spirit, she affirms, along with those of other children he has drawn to the museum, that plays havoc with the pram at night.

THE 1725 CAPTAIN TAYLOR HOUSE
(Plymouth, Massachusetts)

There are some with vision beclouded
Who see not all that they might;
And some, of a finer essence born,
Who see with the inner sight.
—Isabella Banks

As evidenced by the events narrated in the previous chapter, Ric Cone is no stranger to weird phenomena. The Taylor-Trask Museum, for which he serves as both director and curator, is frequently the setting for inexplicable occurrences—enough of them to warrant a chapter of their own (following this one). And yet Ric's acquaintance with the outré goes far beyond willful wax dolls, haunted prams, and a museum which apparently experiences more activity after closing than it does during daylight hours.

Ric Cone resides, and earns his living, in a haunted house. His unique gift shop, the Old North Street Shop (next door to the museum), occupies a portion of the first floor of the 1725 Captain Taylor House. The apartment which he shares with his partner, Yoko, also occupies space on the first floor. On the floor above, Ric and Yoko host the 1725 Captain Taylor Inn, a bed-and-breakfast featuring comfortable rooms furnished with quaint antiques, and views of Plymouth Harbor.

Located on the second oldest street in Plymouth (and therefore one of the oldest streets in America), the Captain Taylor House was built by Juda West shortly after he purchased the land in 1725. Thirty years later Captain Jacob Taylor acquired the property, which remained in his family for more than a century. In 1830 Jacob's grandsons, Jacob and Abner (architects and builders), added to the house and remodeled it according to the fashion of the period. They also built the house next door, now the Taylor-Trask Museum.

Both houses are located on Cole's Hill, site of an ancient Wampanoag Burial Ground and an early graveyard of the Pilgrims. Perhaps this fact, along with the rich and varied history of the two buildings, accounts for the unusual activities which continually occur within their walls.

The story of how Ric came to occupy the Captain Taylor House is fascinating in its own right, in that even though he is not originally from the area, but only vacationed in Plymouth as a teenager, he had always felt drawn toward the property—as if somehow a bond existed between him and the house. Later, when he was living in Dennisport on Cape Cod, whenever he visited Plymouth he would make a point of driving down North Street, though he was not at the time familiar with its history. Long before the opportunity to reside and conduct a business in the Captain Taylor House came about, visions of the house would appear in his dreams. In his own words: "There's an affinity between me and the house, as if I can't ever leave it."

Through a series of coincidences he came to occupy—in an incredibly short span of time—first one section of the old house, then another, and another, almost as if he were meant to dwell, for however brief a period, in every one of the building's several apartments.

It was in the first set of rooms he lived in, in the "newer" half of the house (constructed by Jacob and Abner in 1830 as a mirror image of the original 1725 dwelling), that he began to realize that the house is haunted.

Ric and Yoko noticed that whenever they watched a program on television or played a video that featured loud noises and exceptional violence, the bathroom door would slam shut, sometimes "right in our faces." This happened even when no windows in the house were open that might cause a draft (in fact, the bathroom itself had no window.) And it would happen *only* when they watched a show with violent content.

When, later, they shifted their living quarters to the older side of the house they sometimes felt cold drafts—even in hot weather. And heard noises, such as footsteps. And a woman's voice calling, "Richard? Richard? Are you there?"

More than once Ric has seen the shadow of a man wearing a bulky coat and a wide-brimmed hat shimmer along the walls, in the house's many nooks and crannies.

Several years ago, though it was in the month of June, Ric and Yoko suddenly felt "an incredible cold" in their apartment. Winslow, their Maine Coon, jumped on the bureau and stared at the ceiling—an uncharacteristic behavior for this normally placid cat. And although the 1725 Captain Taylor Inn (located directly above) was vacant at the time, they heard footsteps in the B&B's parlor.

Ric grabbed a flashlight, and with Winslow two or three paces ahead climbed the stairs in the rear to investigate. As he mounted the steps the cold seemed to intensify. Unusual for him, Ric says,

he felt "a great fear." When they reached the top of the stairs Winslow bounded toward the parlor, but balked at the doorway and refused to enter.

Ric hesitated, then entered the room. As he crossed the threshold—hearing footsteps, and with the distinct feeling that he was not alone—the bulb of the flashlight (brand-new, bought just a few days earlier) abruptly died, leaving him in the dark.

He switched on the lights and made a thorough investigation of the empty B&B, but found no evidence of anyone having been there.

When he examined the defective flashlight he discovered that the bulb had fused. A second flashlight, bought at the same time as the other, works perfectly to this day. Strange, that the first flashlight should fail just as Ric crossed the threshold—into a room where phantom footsteps are frequently heard.

When—comfortably ensconced on one of the antique chairs in the parlor of the 1725 Captain Taylor Inn—I interviewed Ric for this book, I asked whether he was concerned that the reputation of his B&B for being haunted might hurt business.

"Not at all," he replied. "It's just an added attraction."

"Have any guests ever reported anything unusual?"

"On one or two occasions, yes. Guests from San Diego who were staying in the back bedroom awoke one night around two a.m. and saw a man standing in their room. He was dressed like a sailor from the 1700's.

"Another time there was a pair of guests, one from America, the other from Greece. I reminded the man from Greece that this is a non-smoking B&B.

"'I'll smoke outside,' he promised. But later, when I smelled smoke and suspected him of smoking inside, he confessed that there was a feeling about the house that made him nervous.

"'Ghosts,' I told him.

"'I know,' he said, and packed up his bags and left."

"What's the strangest thing that's ever happened here?"

Ric thought for a while before saying, "Probably the incident of 'the little girl who wasn't there.'"

"Ah," I said, and settled back in the chair while Ric related the story.

"One evening in July, around 5:30 as usual, I locked the street door to the gift shop. Then I exited through the back into the front door of our apartment. Yoko was taking a shower. When she stepped out, she glanced toward the shop and shouted: 'Ric! You left the shop door open. There's a little girl running around in there.'

"'All the doors are locked,' I assured her. 'As well as all the windows. There's nobody in the shop.'

"'But I saw her,' Yoko insisted. 'A little girl with light brown hair, in a summer dress and no shoes. You must have locked her in the shop.'

"So I went back to the shop and investigated. The street door was still securely fastened. And of course there was nobody in there.

"A few days later we were sitting on the porch, eating Chinese food and chatting with some folks from the Colonial Lantern Tours here in town. I mentioned the incident of 'the little girl who wasn't there'.

"'Describe her,' someone suggested.

"Yoko did, and they said: 'You saw Abigail Townsend. She's been seen before on this street. She died a long time ago from an abscessed tooth.'"

Ric laughed. "When she heard that, Yoko turned white. To this day she doesn't care to talk about the incident."

"What's the scariest thing that's happened?" I asked.

"Well," Ric said, "the most negative feeling I've had—even

12

more so than the intense fear I felt that night when I went upstairs with Winslow to investigate the phantom footsteps—was one evening in August.

"It was dusk, around 7:30 or 8:00; I was in the shop at the cash register. I thought I was alone. But when I happened to glance over to the shelves where we store our loose teas I saw a man standing there. A dark figure half-hidden by the shelves. I couldn't distinguish his features. But I could see that he had on clothing typical of the eighteenth century: a long coat, and boots typical of that period. (I have a background in history and recognized the style.)

"He stood there for seven or eight minutes without moving. I suspected that he might be a shoplifter.

"Finally I said: 'Excuse me. Can I help you?'

"He didn't answer. It was dark in the shop. I moved closer. When I was about three feet away he turned and disappeared behind the shelves."

Ric shrugged. "That was it. He simply vanished. That was the scariest—the most negative—feeling. I felt that something bad had entered the shop. That it was some sort of warning, for him to stand there so long.

"I never saw him again. But it wasn't long after that something else happened. Which—now that I think about it—is probably even more frightening.

"A man and a woman came into the gift shop. The man was immediately noticeable because of the way he was dressed. (For reasons you'll shortly understand I can't describe him in any more detail. But the way he was dressed caused other people to stare.)

"It was a Saturday afternoon and the shop was crowded, with four or five other customers. The man and the woman began to argue. Not loudly, but you could tell they were having an argument. I began to be concerned for my other customers, who were getting uneasy.

"There's a bookcase in the shop where we keep old books. As the man passed in front of it a huge, thick book flew off one of the shelves and landed at his feet, open, with the pages down. The book actually shot off of the shelf, straight out, as if propelled. It was a mammoth book and just missed hitting him by the hair of his nose.

"I wasn't the only one who saw this. Most of the other customers did, too.

"The man stood there, stunned. Then he walked out of the shop, followed by his wife. I know she was his wife because a year later I saw her picture on television, along with his. He's accused of murdering her.

"It's a notorious case. I've confirmed with other shop owners in the area that it was definitely the accused murderer and his wife whom we saw that day. He has a unique face—and was dressed in the unforgettable way I alluded to. The trial is still going on. For that reason, and because it's such a sensitive issue, I'd rather not name the couple. But I'm sure if you read newspapers or watch television you're familiar with the whole thing.

"What I find so chilling is, the book that literally jumped off the shelf as he walked by. It's an old, 1870's bible. At the time I simply picked it up and put it back in its place. But now I kick myself for not taking note of the passage it opened to when it fell at his feet."

postscript

Several chapters from this book, including the one above, were published in 2001 as a 32-page chapbook with the title *Ghosts in Black and White: Some Hauntings in Plymouth County.*

At the time, the trial involving the man who was "noticeable because of the way he was dressed" when he visited the gift shop was still in progress. Now that a verdict has been reached, I can

14

identify the couple as Dr. Richard Sharpe and his wife, Karen. Dr. Sharpe, a wealthy Gloucester dermatologist, was a cross-dresser and therefore readily stood out in a crowd. In the fall of 2001 his plea of innocent by reason of insanity failed, and he was found guilty of murdering his wife.

One cannot help wondering along with Ric Cone: what passage was it that the antique bible opened to, when it shot out of the bookcase and landed at Dr. Sharpe's feet? 🕯

THE WOMAN IN THE WHITE DRESS
(Plymouth, Massachusetts)

Is there ever a maid or widow
Whose love lies under a stone,
Who holds not a ghost to her aching heart,
To cherish and call her own?
—Isabella Banks

or whatever reason, Ric Cone confesses, he has "an urge to tell stories" about the historic figures who have lived at 35 North Street—in the very heart of Plymouth—in the house now known as the Taylor-Trask Museum.

Perhaps this urge is merely the result of Ric's natural talents as an actor. When he first came to the Plymouth area to work, it was as a colonial interpreter for Plimouth Plantation, where for two years he honed his skills as raconteur of the past. Now, as curator and director of the Taylor-Trask Museum, he often portrays in period costume (roughly 1860-1880) Nathaniel Bourne Spooner, who lived in the house for a good portion of the nineteenth century, and who is famous locally for having founded the Plymouth Cordage Company.

Or could there be some other—perhaps "paranormal"—explanation for Ric's passion for representing people from the past?

During a seance at the museum, the noted New England psychic who was conducting it turned to Ric and said, "You have to sit down and listen to what I have to say. You have been brought here to tell the stories of the people who once lived here.

"Things are finding their way back to this house."

Hearing her words, Ric immediately thought of the bundle of old photographs he'd recently purchased in Duxbury. When he showed the photos to someone whose family had once lived in the house, she recognized her mother and aunt in one of them.

"In the early nine-
teenth century," the
psychic went on to
inform him, "you were a
judge. You were kind to
children."

During the seance,
Ric says, he could feel
the presence of "a circle of people grouped around."

"You can almost see the people who once lived here," the
psychic told him.

One day Ric in fact did see something which, he believes,
was the image (or ghost?) of someone who once lived in the house.

The sighting occurred as evening thickened into dusk and an
orange sun sank low in the sky. Ric was seated in the museum
talking with a friend. Outside, a figure walked by the window: a
tall man resembling Abe Lincoln. Ric watched as the image moved
along with what he describes as a ripple effect, "like a pebble in
water."

"Did you see that!" he exclaimed to his friend.

His friend—whom Ric describes as being very religious—
seemed shaken, and reluctant to reply. Finally when pressed he
said: "Maybe I did." After that he declined to speak further about
it, or to mention it again.

Ric has little doubt that the figure—who if in the flesh would
have to be nine feet tall to be seen from that particular vantage
point—was none other than Nathaniel Bourne Spooner.

Other than the pram that changes position at night (and

sometimes during the day), and the apparition of Mr. Spooner, nothing very unusual has occurred in the museum lately—unless you consider what happened last year shortly before Halloween *unusual.*

Ric says that the two weeks prior to Halloween were busy ones at the museum, with about 800 visitors passing through. During the final three days preceding the holiday strange things began to occur, the weirdest involving a feather in a pewter inkwell—an incident witnessed by approximately thirty people.

Suddenly without apparent cause a feather (or quill pen) popped out of the antique inkwell into the air, spun around several times, then fell back to its original position.

Lest you receive the erroneous impression that the hauntings at 35 North Street are recent phenomena, let me conclude this chapter with mention of the woman in the white dress.

I intentionally say "mention" because there is not a whole lot of narrative, and even less plot, to her story. Simply stated, in the past—before the place became a museum—two families residing in the house (at different times) reported seeing a woman in a white dress. She would appear at one of the windows facing the harbor, wipe a tear from her eye, then disappear.

No one seems to know who the woman is (or rather, *was*). Ric, however, has a theory. He believes that the woman in white may be the spirit of the mother of Jacob and Abner Taylor, grieving over the death of her husband, Captain Edward Taylor, who drowned in Plymouth Harbor. *&*

Who's That Tapping on My Shoulder?
(Plymouth, Massachusetts)

In the fall of 2001, just in time for Halloween, Rock Village Publishing came out with *Ghosts in Black and White*, the aforementioned chapbook consisting of a shortened version of the first three chapters of this book, along with "The Black Dog of North Carver" and "A Tale of Two Witches." (Collectors take note: the first printing of *Ghosts in Black and White*, limited to a paltry two hundred and fifty copies, already commands a premium in the rare book market.)

In February of 2002, at Ric's invitation, Yolanda and I spent a night at the 1725 Captain Taylor Bed and Breakfast. As described in a feature article in a recent issue of *Offshore* magazine, the interior of the B&B "looked like an antique shop"—though perhaps it would be more accurate to describe it as "tastefully decorated with antiques," which along with the many paintings and prints hanging on the walls lend a genteel atmosphere to the rooms. Staying at the 1725 Captain Taylor B&B is like being a guest in an early Victorian middle-class household (with modern conveniences of course)—circa 1850 say, though a few of the antiques may date from a later period.

Ric refers to the set of rooms that comprise the B&B as a suite, though they seem grander than that, consisting of a dining room and kitchenette, a living room, two bedrooms and a bath, and a hallway which connects one of the bedrooms and the living room with the rest of the suite. There are two stairways. One leads down to the front door (and an interior door to the gift shop); a second leads to the downstairs where Ric and Yoko have their apartment.

Ric offered us a choice of bedrooms. Although the front room is airy, light, and inviting, we chose the equally cozy bedroom in back, simply because it's closer to the bathroom. An interesting feature of the bedroom door is that it boasts six panels, the top two of which—in lieu of a transom—are actually miniature doors themselves, or shutters, which can be opened or closed to allow for ventilation or privacy.

Despite its reputation for being haunted, the B&B exudes an

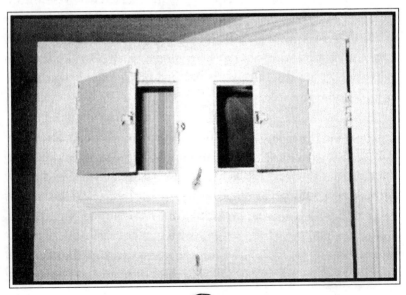

aura of comfort and charm. The only object in it that can even remotely be described as spooky—and that's stretching it—is a painting that hangs next to the bathroom door. *Moonlight on the Waters* by Will Lannin dates from around 1880 and is of the Hudson River School. The scene it depicts is at once serene and eerie: a partially obscured moon above the still waters of a river harbor, with cliffs in the background, a sailboat on the river and other boats docked by the shore, a lodge-type building, and two figures huddled near an open fire.

Yolanda and I arrived in Plymouth late on a Saturday afternoon, just as Ric was closing up the gift shop. He and Yoko accompanied us upstairs to the B&B, and after we'd had a few minutes to settle in, joined us in the living room, where the four of us chatted for nearly two hours. During that time Ric filled us in on events that had transpired since our last visit.

Any fears I might have had that the ghosts of North Street had been quiescent in the past few months were soon put to rest by Ric. He informed me that on one autumn night in particular they—or at least one of them—had been very active indeed. But before I get to *that* story, I'll repeat another that Ric also told us that evening.

It was a story that he had forgotten to tell me previously, when I was gathering material for *Ghosts in Black and White.*

The building that is now the Taylor-Trask Museum used to house a museum of theater arts (established by Franklin Trask, a well-known producer who was instrumental in founding both the Brattle Street Theater and the Priscilla Beach Theater.) The walls of all four rooms of the original museum were covered with photos, mostly of Broadway plays taken by famous New York photographers. Probably because of its Plymouth location (where Pilgrim and other purely New England themes predominate), the museum of theater arts never prospered. When Ric took charge it had been closed for seven years.

"The walls were plastered with photos," Ric told me. "Hundreds and hundreds. They covered every inch of space, like wallpaper, in all four rooms."

The holders that framed the photographs were nailed to the walls, which were of horsehair plaster. At first Ric tried to pull out the nails. But this proved too damaging to the plaster, so he and Yoko ended up driving the nails into the wall—more than a thousand —and plastering over them. It was a tedious, time-consuming process.

As Ric describes it, "We had to carefully remove the photographs, drive the nails in, apply plaster, sand it down, add more plaster, and sand again. Then apply paint: a total of three coats. It took Yoko and me a full three months, working every night that winter—sometimes till well past midnight—to complete just the first three rooms.

"By then our knuckles were scraped raw.

"One night when the project was about three-fourths completed Yoko went home (to our apartment next door) while I continued to work. Sometime around a quarter past eleven I felt a strange sensation on my left shoulder, as if someone were tapping on it. The taps felt firm but not threatening. At first I thought I was experiencing a muscle spasm. But the sensation kept on happening. First one shoulder, then the other. It felt just like someone's finger. First one finger, then two, then three, finally a whole hand, including the thumb.

"I became frightened and began to freak out. I quickly put the tools down and leaving the lights on went to the front door. All the while it felt as though someone was holding on to my right shoulder.

"I locked the door and raced around the back, where there's a space behind the bushes between the two houses. As I ran the hand kept a firm grip on my shoulder. It wasn't until I crossed the property line that the hand let go."

Following that episode Ric was reluctant to go back into the museum, and it was several months before he felt comfortable again working there at night alone. After the new Taylor-Trask Museum opened, visitors occasionally reported the sensation of being touched on the shoulders by phantom fingers, or feeling them brushing against their cheeks.

Ric chuckles when he thinks of all those hundreds of nails he and Yoko pounded back into the walls. "They're like a huge grid," he says, "acting like a spirit magnet."

On a more serious note he mentioned a neighbor, a friend of his, a descendent of the Mayflower who—though originally from the Midwest—felt (like Ric) "that he was drawn here." While staying in an apartment in the back of the building that houses

27

the museum, he was awakened in the middle of the night by a sudden noise. When he went into the dining room to investigate, he discovered that a chair had been pulled out from the table at an angle—the very same angle at which his mother was in the habit of leaving her dining room chair. He felt that her spirit was there with him.

Ric's friend's mother was fond of the singer Ann Murray. Remembering this, the friend bought one of the singer's tapes and, after playing it, placed it on the dining room table. He left the room; when he returned the tape was gone. He has not found it since.

Ric confesses that he, too, feels his own mother's presence in the museum.

When Ric told Yolanda and me of this episode, Yoko was reminded that a couple who had previously lived in the same apartment claimed they had a ghost who frequently whistled. They also reported that a rocking chair, which had been their grandmother's, would rock by itself, and that they would often find a blanket on the chair, though neither of them had put it there.

As indicated earlier, the ghosts on North Street had not been idle since the last time Yolanda and I paid a visit. In fact, one night something occurred that still has people in the neighborhood talking (or, in the case of some of the more timid souls, *whispering*).

It was after nine o'clock on a cold, raw Friday evening in late autumn of the year 2001. Ric had fallen asleep early and was dozing on the couch. Yoko had already gone to bed.

Suddenly Ric heard a noise that woke him: it sounded like some sort of commotion on the porch, where he keeps furniture and other items for sale. Shoeless, wearing only a T-shirt and pants, he grabbed a flashlight and went out to investigate. He encountered a group of about twenty people gathered in the garden of the Taylor-Trask Museum. They were staring in the direction of his shop.

He recognized Joyce, leader of a local tour group, and apologizing for interrupting her tour, asked: "Did you happen to see anyone on my porch?"

"No," she answered. "But we just now saw a lit candle moving around in front of the window inside the shop. Four people saw the flame—with no one holding the candle as it moved around."

Ric thanked her and rushed inside the shop. It was pitch black, and empty, save for a residue of smoke—as if someone had just extinguished a candle. Perhaps strangest of all, the bulb in the window display unit had blown out. Ric flicked on the lights and discovered a colonial-style candle holder—with the wax in it still warm and moist.

The next morning Ric received a phone call from his neighbor, Barbara, who lives in the late-eighteenth-century Captain Russell House across the street. She reported that, during the night, she had seen "a red, beady light moving around inside the shop."

Despite all the uncanny activity that he encounters and has to contend with in the two properties—the 1725 Captain Taylor House and the Taylor-Trask Museum next door—Ric insists that his historic corner of North Street in Plymouth, Massachusetts, is "a very healing place; it gives a warm feeling."

Ric seems to have the same attitude as Dorthy, of the "House of the Five Suicides" in Middleborough, and Richard, who shares his house in Taunton with "A Ghost Named Wendell" (both of whom are featured in *Haunters of the Dusk*)—the sense that the spirits they live with are benevolent.

"I'll never find this kind of peace elsewhere," Ric says, with firm conviction. "The spirits are so in touch. They want to tell us about their lives."

At times, though, the spirits can be difficult, especially when they play pranks. Occasionally they'll hide an object—like the time Ric "misplaced" his keys.

"I have one superstition," Ric told me. "For whatever reason, I believe it's bad luck to place keys on a table. I never, ever, place my keys on a table. Not long ago, while in the museum, I put my keys on an embroided chair and went into the next room for a meeting. When I returned the keys were gone. I looked everywhere, and eventually had everyone searching throughout the museum. The keys were nowhere to be found. Later, I came back into the room and there they were, on the embroided chair where I had originally left them.

"Ramona, the psychic who held a seance in the museum, says that it's the spirits of the kids who like to play tricks. Especially when there's a lot of activity going on, when people are around. But the spirits are by no means malevolent. Whenever something is missing I know eventually I'll find it."

"They play tricks on me, too," Yoko said. "Sometimes they don't want to let me in. Sometimes I have trouble opening the door to the museum."

Ric agreed. "Sometimes the door simply won't open. It has nothing to do with the weather. It happened to me last Halloween. Sometimes the spirits just don't want to let us in."

Then there's the doorbell.

"It's one of those old-fashioned doorbells," Ric said. "The

30

kind that you pull. I was inside the museum one day, when I heard the doorbell ring. I went to the door. No one was there. I went back inside. The bell rang again. I went to the door once more, and again no one was there. Out of curiosity I pulled the bell. It wouldn't ring!

"But when I went back inside the bell started ringing, and after that it wouldn't stop."

I asked Ric if the pram had been misbehaving lately.

He shook his head. "It hasn't moved since last fall. Things have been fairly quiet this winter."

"Fairly quiet," too, is the way I would describe our stay at the B&B.

After an excellent seafood dinner at a local restaurant (with a romantic view of Plymouth Harbor), the four of us returned to North Street to settle in for the night. Ric and Yoko warned us that the ancient heating system was noisy and might keep us awake. It didn't. I don't think I've ever spent a more comfortable—or quieter—night in a bed-and-breakfast.

Before Yolanda and I retired for the evening Winslow came up for a visit. He remained for about half an hour. Strangely, he acted as if he was spooked by something. Yolanda and I both noticed it. He seemed ill at ease—not with us (we've always got along well with our favorite Maine Coon; and after all, he was there at his own volition, and the experience of being in the B&B was nothing new; he usually spends time with guests) but at something . . . intangible.

When the next morning we mentioned Winslow's odd behavior to Ric, he told us that the cat sometimes, unaccountably, acts like that—that he seems to be acutely aware when there's "something" present.

Other than Winslow's disquietude, nothing untoward occurred

during our stay at the 1725 Captain Taylor House. True, Yolanda says that she was awakened at ten minutes to five Sunday morning by the sound of a radio playing (no one else heard it). And Sunday morning, as we were enjoying the excellent breakfast that Ric and Yoko prepared for us, Ric wanted to know whether we'd called out to him the previous evening. (We hadn't.)

Shortly after leaving us for the evening, Ric said, he'd distinctly heard a woman's voice call, "Richard." Though he knows that we refer to him as "Ric," he thought that it was Yolanda calling down, that perhaps we were in need of something. He went on to say that he called up to us, quite loudly, but we failed to answer.

Even though at that time Yolanda and I were chatting quietly in the living room, we didn't hear Ric call up to us. Strange. But then...after all, this was North Street. ⚰

THE BLACK DOG OF NORTH CARVER
(Carver, Massachusetts)

If ever you find yourself driving along Route 44 in North Carver, Massachusetts —perhaps on your way to visit the Taylor-Trask Museum in Plymouth—take a few minutes to turn into the drive

at 164 Plymouth Street and visit the Cranberry Book Barn. Better yet, don't wait for chance to take you there; plan a special trip. It's worth the pilgrimage.

As its name suggests, the Cranberry Book Barn is a classic example of that rural New England icon, a weathered barn by the side of the road which has been converted into an antique shop or, in this instance, a bookstore featuring used, rare, and out-of-print books.

Too often these ancient buildings are damp, musty, and ill-lit. Or the opposite: dry, dusty, and festooned with cobwebs. Not so the Cranberry Book Barn. Within its cozy and well-lit interior the shelves are neatly arranged, easy to browse, and—most important of all—mold- and dust-free.

If I sound like an ad for the place, why not? I'm a satisfied customer. I've discovered a number of absorbing books there: local histories, nature guides, and—of prime interest to readers of this book—collections of forgotten ghost stories.

However, the most engaging ghost associated with the Cranberry Book Barn does not reside between the covers of a book, but within the building itself. For the Cranberry Book Barn is haunted.

The house at 164 Plymouth Street, built in 1792, belonged at one time to members of the Braddock family. In *Memories of North Carver Village* (published in 1977), Ellsworth C. Braddock wrote about the history of the area and in particular about the families who lived in North Carver in the early decades of the twentieth century. I mention this because of an incident that occurred in 1994, shortly after Colleen Preston moved into the house and established the barn as a bookstore.

A man entered the barn with a book to sell: a huge leather-bound bible with an old-fashioned latch. When Colleen opened the bible her glance fell upon the name inscribed within: Harold Braddock.

A coincidence, no doubt. But one that calls to mind similar goings-on in the Taylor-Trask Museum and the 1725 Captain

Taylor House—incidents involving an old bible and objects returning (willfully?) to their former haunts.

Old bibles notwithstanding, it was Colleen's mother, Doris Kelly, who first saw the barn's resident ghost. One day when she was in charge of the store she saw a black dog dash behind one of the glass bookcases. Thinking she had seen Mocha, Colleen's mixed shepherd and Lab—whom she'd assumed to be outdoors—Doris went looking for the dog. She searched throughout the store, even the attic, until happening to glance out a window she saw Mocha tethered outside.

Colleen dismissed her mother's account of the incident—until something similar happened to *her*. Stationed behind the cash register, with customers in the store, she glimpsed—out of the corner of her eye—a black dog passing behind the glass bookcase. At the same time, she saw her own dog, Mocha, tied outside.

Colleen's daughter Kelly (who happens to be a vet) was skeptical when she heard both her mother and grandmother talk about the mysterious black dog that would suddenly appear, then as suddenly vanish. She's still skeptical, I'm told—though there was the time when, apparently, she saw something in the barn and exclaimed: "What dog was that that just went by?"

Whenever the black dog makes an appearance, it always vanishes in the same spot: just as it enters a recent addition to the barn—at the exact line where the old barn used to end.

Although Colleen cannot say for sure why the ghost of a black dog haunts her bookstore, she does have a theory that may account for its presence.

38

Her daughter Kelly was talking to an older resident in town one day and—without mentioning the barn's canine specter—learned that back in the 1950's a man kept a black Labrador retriever in the barn. Unfortunately he was known to mistreat the dog. Feeling sorry for it, the neighborhood kids would often sneak into the barn to feed it and otherwise try to make its life more bearable.

Oddly, when Mocha died two years after Colleen opened her bookstore, the ghostly dog stopped appearing, and Colleen and her mother soon forgot about it. For several years the only dog on the premises was a small dog owned by Kelly. Then Colleen acquired Sandy, a friendly shepherd. And the black dog began to be seen again.

Colleen believes that the ghost of the mistreated dog is seeking a kindred spirit, that it felt comfortable with the large, friendly Mocha, and feels at home with the equally amiable Sandy. 🐾

As for the ultimate reasons why we read these stories, that tiresome, unanswerable question has already been raised too many times. That we enjoy them is enough. The reasons remain as perverse and mysterious as the stories themselves.
— *Jack Sullivan,* Elegant Nightmares

FROM THE ARCHIVES

43

BURIED BONES AND HIDDEN TREASURE
(Hallowell, Maine)

fossick. 1. To search for gold, especially by reworking washings or waste piles. 2. To rummage or search, especially for a possible profit. —The American Heritage Dictionary of the English Language

Whenever possible, I like to travel throughout the New England countryside and stop at the many small libraries and historical societies, to fossick through ancient volumes of local lore in search of forgotten ghost stories.

Recently I found such a story in Hallowell, Maine.

As Maine's smallest city, Hallowell—with a population of 2700—is scarcely larger than many a small town. The Hubbard Free Library, a beautiful stone edifice, was built in 1880. The railroad track runs along behind it. Once, I was told, a train derailed and crashed through the library wall. No such untoward incident occurred the day I visited. But something almost as exciting did happen: my discovery of a crumbling old book

45

chockful of legends and folklore.

Legends and Otherwise of Hallowell and Loudon Hill by Edward Preble Norton was published in 1923, by the Press of Charles E. Nash & Son in Augusta, Maine.

Norton, who was born in 1838, died in 1892. The book is a compilation of columns and sketches he wrote for a local newspaper. Although I didn't have an opportunity to read the entire book (which, as a rare antiquarian treasure, cannot be taken from the library) I was able to skim through most of it and to extract its most fascinating story, which—with considerable abridgment—I have reproduced below.

"A LEGEND OF LOUDON HILL RELATING TO PIERRE SORENCIE"

by
Edward Preble Norton
[The story, which originally appeared in
The Hallowell Register on October 19, 1889,
is narrated by "an old resident" of Loudon Hill.]

B uilding the new sidewalk on the old disused road from Water to Greenville Street brings to remembrance the time when the road was in use. Very few have an idea why it was abandoned, but I can give an explanation.

The adventure I am about to relate, I have never told to anyone before, but the improvements going on in the old street, and a little song my boy was singing last night,—

"In the sky the bright stars glittered,
On the bank the pale moon shone,
And 'twas from Aunt Dinah's quilting party,
I was seeing Nellie home."

46

recall it so strongly, that I am inclined to give the public a history of the matter.

It had been reported a number of times that a queer-looking old man had been seen occasionally, walking on that street evenings. No one paid him much attention, supposing him to be perhaps a stray sailor. I thought I would like to see the old fellow, and soon had a chance. One evening I went to a husking bee. When it was over I found myself walking home with a girl.

Our road was through the old road, and when we were about half-way down I noticed that she seemed chilly and there seemed to be a draught of cold wind coming up the street, so we both shivered. Then we saw, a little ways ahead, an old gentleman dressed in knee-breeches, wide-skirted coat, and a three-cornered hat, walking slowly along with his hands clasped behind him.

I didn't think anything strange of his dress, as some of the old men still clung to the dress of Revolutionary times.

We soon caught up with him, and as we were passing I said: "Good evening, Sir."

"Good evening, young man, and when you have escorted the young lady safely home, you will do me a great favor by coming back here, if I can trouble you so much. I would like to talk with you."

"All right, sir, I will come."

When we reached the young lady's home she said, "Surely you're not going back there? That old man seemed so weird and uncanny."

I told her that as I had given my word I must return. And I didn't believe he meant harm.

"Well," she said, "if you're so determined I can say nothing more. But I shall wait here on the porch. Do not fail to come to me as soon as possible, that I may be assured of your safety."

I promised, and sealed the promise with a kiss, then hurried back and found the old man about where we had passed him. "If

I can be of any assistance to you, sir, I am ready."

"Let us sit down on this log. I have a story to tell, and wish you to do something for me. I will make it for your interest. It is not often that the privilege is given me to converse with a living man."

A *lunatic*, thought I.

"Not so. I am not what you think, young man."

I was astonished at having my thoughts taken up as though I had spoken. He raised his head, and turning his dark eyes on me said: "Listen, I would do you no harm, and indeed it would be impossible to do so if I wished. I assure you that there is naught to fear from me.

"My name was Pierre Sorencie. I was a native of a small village in Canada, and part soldier, part trader, was in the service of the Marquis Vaudreuil de Carnegal, Governor-General of New France. Myself, with a party of St. Francois Indians, were encamped in this ravine not far from where we are now sitting, when a party of English soldiers in a bateau going up the river to Fort Halifax fired on us with a small canon they carried. It was a fatal shot for me, and wounded two of my Indians.

"My comrades fled, carrying with them a large sum of money belonging to me, which they buried not far from here, as I will show you. When the boat was out of sight they returned and buried my body. What I want of you is to dig up my bones, take them to the nearest priest, and have them placed in consecrated ground; in return I will show you where the hoard of money is buried, which will amply reward you."

I suppose my hair was standing straight up. However, I signified my assent.

"Then," said he, "there is a shovel behind this log, left by some laborer. Take it, and dig as I show you."

I found the shovel; we went across the road and part way up the south bank, when he stopped.

48

"Dig there," he said, pointing out the place.

It didn't take me long to throw out a big pile of dirt, as I was very much excited. Soon my shovel struck something hard. Picking it up, I saw that it was an iron ball, what I should call a large size grapeshot.

"The ball that killed me," said the old man. "Be careful now."

I worked slowly and soon found what looked like the remains of a blanket, enclosing a number of bones, among which I could distinguish a jaw-bone and part of a skull. It came to me afterwards: how clearly I could see things, although it was a dark night in October.

The old gentleman looked at the few fragments and said, "That is all that is left of the human body after a hundred years. Of what account would man be, if there were no hereafter?"

I took the bones, placed them carefully under a small pine bush as he directed, intending to take them to the priest the next day.

"Now I will show you the money." He led the way out to the south end of Greenville Street as it then was, on top of Wharf Hill, and as near as I could judge, four or five rods into the woods, it being dense woods there at that time.

"Stick your shovel there and leave it till you have seen buried all that remains of Pierre Sorencie, then come back and dig, and you will find the money."

I was about to push the shovel into the ground as directed, when I stumbled and fell, my head striking the hard steel of the shovel. I remember seeing all kinds of stars and then things turned black.

When I picked myself up—it could not have been but a few minutes after my fall—it was dark as a pocket, the old man was gone, I could not find the shovel, and at last, badly bruised, and a great deal scared, I made my way out of the woods into the main road.

49

Having no idea of the time, but realizing that I must keep my promise and return to the girl, I turned my steps in that direction. Sure enough, she was there and in rather an unnerved state of mind, which did not improve when she saw me covered with dirt and blood.

"What has happened?"

I told her, just as I have told you.

Thoroughly frightened, she said: "I wish you had listened to my advice and had nothing to do with such business. No good ever comes of it."

The next day I was too lame to move around much, and it rained. But the day after, I went to find the old man's bones. But not a trace could I find. The heavy rains had made havoc of the spot, and there had been a landslide. Pierre Sorencie was buried again, and I could not tell where to dig. As for the money, I hunted all day, but could not locate the place or find the shovel, and at last gave it up, and should have thought it an illusion, had it not been for the grapeshot, which I had in my pocket. I have it now, and will give it to you to show any of the curious, who care to see the memento.

I never saw the old man again, but he was seen by others. The road acquired a bad name. Horses going through would shy, without apparent reason. People began to avoid it, and soon it was in a state of neglect. Finally the rains gullied it out badly and it was not repaired.

Since the new sidewalk has been built, I have heard that a queer old man has been seen, pacing up and down, after the dusk of evening.

One other legend of ghosts and buried treasure concerns Maine's smallest city.

"In a former day Hallowell throve as a port and shipbuilding center, but now little vestige of her quondam activity remains, save for a Kidd legend," wrote Richard M. Dorson in his book of New England folklore, *Jonathan Draws the Long Bow*. It seems that the notorious pirate, Captain Kidd, was quite active along the coast of Maine, and once, "under a ravine on the Chelsea side of the Kennebec River, which, due to some air current, is cased in a drift of fog, the Captain buried part of his loot; and there, amid the phantoms of ships sunk in distant waters that return on the tide, swells the sail of Kidd on foggy days and wintry nights. For the Captain and his ghostly crew have returned to watch their treasure."

The motif of ghosts revealing the location of buried money is not uncommon. For example, *Shadows and Cypress: Southern Ghost Stories*, a collection compiled by Alan Brown, contains a number of them, the most interesting being "Uncle Isum's Treasure," a story of the Civil War. And the motif of troubled spirits unable to rest until given proper burial is even more common. The legend of Pierre Sorencie and his buried wealth nicely combines both.

With not just one, but *two* legends concerning buried treasure, Hallowell, Maine, seems like a good place in which to spend some leisure time. Who knows? Some rainy, foggy evening as you stroll alone along a wooded byway or path along the river's edge, someone, some *thing*, may accost you—with a tale to tell.

BLISS ON NANTUCKET
(Nantucket, Massachusetts)

The ghost liked the stairs best, where people passed quickly and occasionally, holding their feelings in suspense between the closing of one door and the opening of another.—Fay Weldon, "Watching Me, Watching You"

For many years now William Root Bliss, a regional writer of the late nineteenth and early twentieth century, has been a favorite author of mine. He wrote about areas I'm familiar with—such as Plymouth County, Massachusetts, and in particular, Wareham, the town in which I was born, and where I grew up and went to school. And where I heard my first ghost story.

Even more compelling, Bliss wrote—in a calm, sedate, reflective manner—about the type of things that interest me: nature, and local history, and New England legends and lore. In the chapter that follows this one I'll include one or two stories he recorded about witches in Plymouth County. But here I'd like to share with you (in a somewhat abridged version) something from

September Days on Nantucket, first published more than a hundred years ago, in 1902. Although the story betrays a degree of cultural insensitivity —a pattern all too common in the past—toward the plight of Nantucket's original (i.e., Indian) inhabitants, I believe it is worth repeating, both as history and as entertainment.

"OLD HOUSES AND GHOSTS"
by
William Root Bliss

This sunny forenoon we went to examine an old house which is said to be the oldest house on the island. Jethro Coffin built it in the year 1686, when he was twenty-three years old and had just married Mary Gardner, a child of sixteen years. He braced the frame of the house with ship knees so that winter gales should not sag it, and he built on the face of the chimney a brick device in the shape of a horseshoe, so that good luck should come to it. But this token has not saved the house from "decay's effacing fingers." It stands dilapidated and solitary in a grassy field, and in all details it reveals the hard features of a time when men and women were so poor that they were compelled to earn their living by continuous labor. The house is empty, like the abandoned shell of the chambered nautilus; those who lived in it having left long ago their "low-vaulted past" to build homes in some wider sphere of life than any that existed on Nantucket.

As a specimen of a dwelling-house in colonial times it is uninteresting. It is partly in ruins, it is small, ungainly in proportions, and hardly worth the attention given to.

Nevertheless, as one of the few curiosities which the islanders have to show, it receives many visits from summer people. They notice a little opening close to the front door, a peephole through which persons within the house inspected those who knocked on the door for admission; it was especially useful to ascertain if an Indian caller was drunk, for drunkfullness was the usual condition of the Indian population of Nantucket. The front door opens into a small space. On the right hand and on the left are doors leading into large rooms; and over these in the second story are two similar rooms, reached by winding stairs supported against the chimney around which the house was built. The ceilings are low, the frame-posts are in sight, and the fireplaces are wide enough to receive cordwood in its full length.

Some country houses of the seventeenth century contained secret closets and haunted rooms, as described in the ghost story told by Tennyson, based on a legend related by James Russell Lowell of a house, near the place where he lived, which was vexed by—

"A footstep, a low throbbing in the walls,
A noise of falling weights that never fell,
Weird whispers, bells that rang without a hand,
Door-handles turned when none was at the door,
And bolted doors that opened of themselves."

Everybody who has a lingering love for the marvelous likes to see these places. Behind the chimney of Jethro's house was a secret closet which has a story to tell. One day when he was absent, and his wife and baby were spending an afternoon with a neighbor, a drunken Indian entered the house, ascended to the garret, and there fell asleep. At midnight he awoke, and while moving about in the dark garret the floor opened and he dropped into the closet below. He crept out into an adjoining room and began to sharpen his knife on the hearthstones. Mrs. Jethro was awakened by the strange noises, and seizing her babe she fled across the fields to her father's house, pursued by the Indian; but as nothing tragical occurred, the story is not so thrilling as it should be.

If it is true, as Longfellow has said, that "all houses in which men have lived and died are haunted houses," it is also true that the sound of a knife whetted on a hearthstone may be heard at midnight in this ghostly abode of the past.

postscript

Three or four months after recording the above, I was thumbing through *Colonial Architecture of Cape Cod, Nantucket, and Martha's Vineyard*, a book by Alfred Easton Poor originally published in 1932 and reprinted (by Dover Publications) in 1970. The book contains virtually no text but instead features "217 photographs and measured drawings." The lead photograph, which serves as a full-page frontispiece, is captioned "Doorway of the Oldest House on Nantucket" "Date 1686" and identified as "Nantucket, Jethro Coffin House." In the photo, the house appears much as described by Bliss thirty years earlier: "dilapidated and solitary."

In a later section the book features photographs of the bedroom fireplace and parlor fireplace (both in sad disrepair) and also detailed drawings of each.

Truly, if the photographs are any indication, the Jethro Coffin House is haunted—if by nothing else than by the past. (A more recent photograph of the house, which appeared in the December 2001 issue of *Cape Cod Life*, shows it to be in excellent condition.) &

TALES OF TWO WITCHES

(Plymouth County, Massachusetts)

Many a New England village has had its witch, its haunted house, its graveyard ghost, and its goblin stories
—William Root Bliss

The story of the Jethro Coffin house, in the preceding chapter, has a ring of authenticity. The events as told probably really did happen. And late-night visitors to the house probably did actually hear—if only in their imaginations—the sound of a knife being whetted on a hearthstone. Though subtle (or perhaps *because* of its subtlety), it has the power to send a slight but slippery shiver up and down the spine.

The following little tales, on the other hand, have all the trappings of folklore: stories once believed by credulous listeners, but not to be taken literally by today's sophisticated readers. Even so they have their merits, for the student of oral traditions, and for the casual reader as well.

57

from "Old Colony Witch Stories"
by
William Root Bliss

There are two women, descended from one of the English settlers of the Plymouth colony, who tell witch stories and believe in the existence of witches, or of old women who can exercise a supernatural power over others.

"After you pass Carver Green on the old road from the bay to Plymouth," said one of these women, "you will see a green hollow in a field. It is Witches' Hollow, and is green in winter and summer, and on moonlit nights witches have been seen dancing on it to the music of a fiddle played by an old black man. In a small house near the hollow, a little old woman lived who was a witch; she went by the name of Old Betty, and she danced on the green with the devil as a partner.

"There was an old man who lived in that neighborhood by himself; he was kind to Betty, giving her food and firewood. After a while he got tired of her and told her she must keep away. One day he caught her there and put her in a bag, and locked the bag in a closet, and put the key in his pocket, and went away to his work. While he was gone, she got out of the bag and unlocked the door. Then she got his pig, dog, cat, and rooster, put them into the bag, put the bag in the closet and hid herself.

"When the man came home the animals in the bag were making a dreadful noise. 'Ah, ha! Old Betty, there you are!' said the man. He took the bag and dashed it on his doorstone, and the old woman laughed and cried out, 'You ain't killed Old Betty yet!'"

The old women who told the witch stories said that their grandmother had been personally acquainted with two witches, in the last century. One of these was named Deborah Borden,

58

called at that day "Deb Burden," who was supposed to have caused a great deal of mischief in Wareham, Rochester, and Middleborough.

"Once Deb came to Thankful Haskell's in Rochester, and sot by the fire, and her daughter, fourteen year old, was sweeping the room, and she put the broom under Deb's chair. You can't insult a witch more than that, 'cause a broomstick is what they ride on when they go off to mischief. [And brooms were believed to be effective in warding off witches or other evil spirits.]

"Deb was mad as a March hare, and she cussed the child. Next day the child was taken sick, and all the doctors gin her up, and they sent for old Dr. Bemis of Middleborough; he put on his spectacles and looked at her, and said he, 'This child is bewitched; go, somebody, and see what Deb is up to.'

"Mr. Haskell got on his horse and rode to Deb's house; there was nobody in but a big black cat; this was the devil, and witches always leave him to take care of the house when they go out. Mr. Haskell looked around for Deb, and he saw her down to the bottom of the garden by a pool of water, and she was making images out of clay and sticking in pins. As quick as he saw her he knew what ailed the child; so he laid his whip around her shoulders good, and said, 'Stop that, Deb, or you shall be burnt alive!' She whimpered, and the black cat came out and growled and spread his tail, but Mr. Haskell laid on the whip, and at last she screamed, 'Your young one shall git well!' and that child began to mend right off. The black cat disappeared all of a suddint and Mr. Haskell thought the earth opened and took him in."

You may be tempted to dismiss the above accountings as mere hogwash. Before doing so, however, consider this: the women who told the stories, and who obviously believed in the power of witches, lived at a time that lay midway between the present and the Salem Witch Trials. It wasn't all that long ago that people, both men and women, were burned, hanged, or otherwise put to death for practicing witchcraft. 🜚

A Haunted Quarry
(Holyoke, Massachusetts)

*"If a ghost was to appear to me I wouldn't be afraid of him,"
said Grandmother Brown; "and if some night some of you children
see a ghost, you just tell me. I would know, if a ghost came to me,
he either wanted help, or came to warn me; and I should just ask
him what he wanted. Oh, there's no need of bein' afraid of a
ghost."*— What They Say in New England

When I was a boy—some half century ago—when asked,
"What're you doing?" my friends and I would sometimes
reply: "Nothing. Just messin' around."

"Just messin' around" meant that although you were playing,
you weren't playing at anything in particular. You might spend
an entire morning or even an entire day just messin' around. More
often, though, just messin' around would develop into a more
purposeful activity—such as building a tree hut from scraps of
wood, or heading out to the nearest cranberry bog to hunt for
arrowheads, or scouring the roadsides for returnable bottles. (The

quart-size bottles were worth five cents, the smaller sizes two cents. The money thus obtained went a long way to supplement my twenty-five cents a week allowance.)

The other day I found myself in the history room of a local library just messin' around, when I came upon a peculiar little book with the fetching title, *What They Say in New England: A Book of Signs, Sayings, and Superstitions.*

The bulk of the book—collected by Clifton Johnson and published in 1896— consists of folkloric material as described in the subtitle. However, Johnson devoted a small section of the book to miscellaneous items that didn't fall into any particular category, including the excerpt from "Dealing with Ghosts" which I've appropriated as an epigram for this chapter; and a brief story about a haunted quarry— "Tim Felt's Ghost"—worth repeating.

Incidentally, "Dealing with Ghosts" concludes with an addendum by Johnson to Grandmother Brown's declaration, as follows: "If a ghost appeared to a person, the proper words in which to address it were, 'What, in the name of God, do you want?'"

What, in the name of God, one might ask, does Tim Felt's ghost want?

"TIM FELT'S GHOST"
by
Clifton Johnson

Connected with the Ireland Parish district of the city of Holyoke, Massachusetts, is a famous ghost story, which runs as follows: In the old days there lived on "Back Street" a Mr. Felt. One fall he sowed a field of rye. The rye came up well, and in the spring was looking green and thrifty. He was therefore the more disturbed at the frequent visits of Neighbor Hummerston's geese to the said field.

Mr. Felt had a quick temper, and this sort of thing was too much for him. He caught the whole flock one day, killed them, and then wended his way to Deacon Hummerston to inform him what he had done, and where his geese were to be found.

This and other acts showed his hasty temper and savage disposition, and brought him into disrepute among his neighbors. He often cruelly beat his horses and cattle, and there were times when he served the members of his family in the same way.

He had a son, Timothy by name, a dull-witted fellow, who was slow of comprehension, and in his work made many mistakes. This was a cause of frequent anger to his father, who on such occasions would strike Tim to the earth with whatever implement he happened to have in hand,—a hoe, a rake, or a pitchfork, perchance. These attacks sometimes drove Tim from home; but, after a few days' absence, necessity would bring him back again. At last, however, he disappeared, and was seen no more; and a little later the Felts moved West.

In building the New Haven and Northhampton canal, a great deal of limestone was used. On Mr. Felt's farm was a ledge of this rock, and the company soon had a quarry there. The overseer was a rough, ill-tempered fellow; and it was not long before he had trouble with his workmen, and they all left him. That brought work to a standstill, and the overseer was at his wit's end to find some way out of his difficulty.

One night, shortly after the men left, the overseer, on his way home from the corner store, quite late, saw a dark figure standing on the limestone ledge, outlined against the sky. The overseer stood still, his frightened gaze riveted on the stranger. Presently he broke the silence by asking, "Who are you? and what is your business?"

The spectre replied, "My name is Timothy Felt, and my bones

63

are under where I now stand. I was killed by my father four years ago, and if you will blast this rock you will find my bones."

This story ran through all the country round, and created great excitement. Every day, for some time afterwards, loads of people, not only from Ireland Parish, but from towns quite distant, wended their way thither, inquiring the way to the "ghost place;" and when night came on people would make a long detour rather than pass the spot, and run the risk of meeting Tim's uneasy spirit. Money was raised to continue the quarrying until Tim's skeleton should be brought to light, but no bones were found; and after the overseer had gotten out what stone he wanted, the work lagged and was discontinued. ₿

MEDLEY IN CONNECTICUT
(Stratford, Middletown, and the Thimble Islands)

Who, in the dark, has not had the feeling of some thing *behind him—and, in spite of his conscious reasoning, turned to look?*
— Arthur B. Reeve, The Best Ghost Stories

One of the "keepers" I landed the other day, while fishing through the shelves of the Cranberry Book Barn in North Carver, Massachusetts, is a peculiar little volume burdened with the immodest—and inaccurate—title, *The Best Ghost Stories.*

Like many cheaply produced collections of ghost stories, this little tome contains more dross than gold. Roughly four out of five of the ghastly tales reprinted on its yellowing pages can be described as "the usual suspects," such as Daniel De Foe's "The Apparition of Mrs. Veal" or Edward Bulwer-Lytton's "The Haunted and the Haunters," both long in the public domain. Without exerting myself too strenuously I can—while remaining seated at my desk—reach out and touch a half dozen anthologies which contain at least one, and most probably both, of the aforementioned chestnuts.

Ah, but the remaining twenty per cent of the stories! Real gems, all of them. For instance, "Dey Ain't No Ghosts," by Ellis Parker Butler: a story narrated in dialect which, though not (in my opinion) offensive, might be considered by some to be demeaning. In any case, "Dey Ain't No Ghosts" is an effective, highly original Halloween story—one, however, unlikely to be reprinted in these days of hypersensitive political correctness.

Another "story" (more accurately, an article encompassing a number of tales and legends) is "Banshees," an encapsulated essay on the tradition of the banshee in Ireland. Reading it, I wanted to hop the next plane to Ireland to spend a night in one of that country's many haunted castles.

The editor, Arthur B. Reeve, concludes *The Best Ghost Stories* with a lengthy chapter entitled "Some Real American Ghosts." These stories, culled from old newspapers, were presumably in the public domain when the book first appeared (whenever *that* was; the book contains no copyright page or date of publication). Some of them are quite interesting. Below, I've reprinted a section which contains a trio of tales consistent with the theme of hauntings in New England.

"GHOSTS IN CONNECTICUT"
(from the New York *Sun*, Sept. 1, 1885)

"There is as much superstition in New England today as there was in those old times when they slashed Quakers and built bonfires for witches." It was a New York man who gave expression to this rather startling statement. He has been summering in Connecticut, and he avers that his talk about native superstition is founded on close observation. Perhaps it is; anyhow he regaled the *Times's* correspondent with some entertaining incidents which he claims establish the truth of his somewhat astonishing theories.

Old Stratford, the whitewashed town between this place and Bridgeport, made famous by mysterious "rappings" many years ago, and more recently celebrated as the scene of poor Rose Clark Ambler's strange murder, is much concerned over a house which the almost universal verdict pronounces "haunted."

The family of Elihu Osborn lives in this house, and ghosts have been clambering through it lately in a wonderfully promiscuous fashion. Two or three families were compelled to vacate the premises before the Osborns, proud and skeptical, took possession of them. Now the Osborns are hunting for a new home.

Children of the family have been awakened at midnight by visitors which persisted in shaking them out of bed; Mrs. Osborn has been confronted with ghostly spectacles, and through the halls and vacant rooms strange footsteps are frequently heard when all the family are trying to sleep; sounds loud enough to arouse every member of the household. Then the manifestations sometimes change to moanings and groanings sufficiently vehement and pitiful to distract all who hear them.

Once upon a time, perhaps a dozen years ago, Jonathan Riggs lived in this house, and as the local gossip asserts, Riggs caused the death of his wife by his brutal conduct and then swallowed poison to end his own life. The anniversary of the murderous month in the Riggs family has arrived and the manifestations are so frequent, and so lively that "the like has never been seen before," as is affirmed by a veteran Stratford citizen.

There is no shadow of doubt in Stratford that the spirits of the Rigges are spryly cavorting around their former abode.

Over at the Thimble Islands, off Stony Creek, is an acre or two of soil piled high on a lot of rocks. The natives call it Frisbe Island. Not more than a hundred yards off shore it contains a big bleak-looking house which was built about twenty years ago to serve as a summer hotel when Connecticut capitalists were deep in schemes to tempt New Yorkers to this part of the Sound shore to spend their summers. New Yorkers declined to be tempted, and the old house is rapidly approaching decay.

It has recently assumed a peculiar interest for the residents of Stony Creek. Midnight lights have suddenly appeared in all its windows, fitfully flashing up and down like the blaze in the Long Island lighthouses. Ghosts! This is the universal verdict. Nobody disputes it. Once or twice a hardy crew of local sailors have volunteered to go out and investigate the mystery, but when the time for the test has arrived, there somehow have always been reasons for postponing the excursion. Cynical people profess to believe that practical jokers are at the root of the manifestations, but such a profane view is not widely entertained among the good people who have their homes at Stony Creek.

Over near Middletown is a farmer named Edgar G. Stokes, a gentleman who is said to have graduated with honor in a New England college more than a quarter of a century ago. He enjoys, perhaps, the most notable bit of superstition to be found anywhere in this country, in or out of Connecticut.

He owns the farm on which he lives, and it is valuable; not quite so valuable though as it once was, for Mr. Stokes's eccentric disposition has somewhat changed the usual tactics that farmers pursue when they own fertile acres. The average man clears his soil of stones; Mr. Stokes has been piling rocks all over his land.

Little by little the weakness—or philosophy—has grown upon him; and not only from every part of Middlesex County, but from every part of this state he has been accumulating wagonloads of pebbles and rocks. He seeks for no peculiar stone either in shape, color, or quality. If they are stones that is sufficient. And his theory is that stones have souls—souls, too, that are not so sordid and earthy as the souls that animate humanity. They are souls purified and exalted. In the rocks are the spirits of the greatest men who have lived in past ages, developed by some divinity until they have become worthy of their new abode. Napoleon Bonaparte's soul inhabits a stone, so does Hannibal's, so does Cæsar's, but poor plebeian John Smith and William Jenkins, they never attained such immortality.

Farmer Stokes has dumped his rocks with more or less reverence all along his fields, and this by one name and that by another he knows and hails them all. A choice galaxy of the distinguished lights of the old days are in his possession, and just between the burly bits of granite at the very threshold of his home is a smooth-faced crystal from the Rocky Mountains. This stone has no soul yet. The rough, jagged rock on its left is George Washington. The granite spar on the right is glorified with the spirit of good Queen Bess.

The smooth-faced crystal one of these days is to know the bliss of swallowing up the spirit of good farmer Edgar Garton Stokes.

It was not until recently that mystified neighbors obtained the secret of the vast accumulation of rough stones on the Stokes farm. Mr. Stokes has a family. They all seem to be intelligent, practical business people. There may be a will contested in Middletown one of these days.

Admittedly, the little piece about farmer Stokes and his stones does not, in the strictest sense, qualify as a *ghost story*. But living as I do in a section of town known as Rock Village (and my wife and I having recently had our old Formica kitchen countertops replaced with new granite ones) I couldn't resist including it.

The writer of the article assumed an amused, condescending tone toward Stokes and implied that his monomania might, upon his demise, lead to a law suit based on "soundness of mind," or lack of it.

All well and good. But my sympathies lie with Edgar Garton Stokes. Throughout the ages, peoples of many lands have recognized a numinous quality in rocks and stones. Indeed, the granite outcrop from which Rock Village derives its name was once a gathering place for the Wampanoags, and in the late nineteenth and early twentieth centuries it served as a meeting place for the revivalist movement.

And, I must confess, though the property on which I reside consists mostly of rocks and gravel, I have been known upon occasion to add to the stones, through acquisitions from elsewhere either found or purchased. *ð*

EVIL ON THE SEAS
(New Shoreham—Block Island—Rhode Island)

In a previous book—*Haunters of the Dusk*—I recounted a strange tale told to me and my wife one foggy evening in the parlor of the Blue Dory Inn on Block Island. It was while researching the background for "A Pathway Through the Roses: The Legend of Headless Alice" that I first encountered stories about a notorious offshore light that has haunted the island for years.

Though I touched upon the legend of the Palatine Light in *Haunters* (in a rather sketchy fashion), I am pleased to once again include it here in this latest collection of New England ghost stories, not only in greater detail, but in a version somewhat different from the account I originally discovered.

This version is taken from *Myths & Legends of Our Own Land* by Charles M. Skinner, published in 1896.

"Block Island and the Palatine"
by
Charles M. Skinner

Block Island, or Manisees, is an uplift of clayey moorland between Montauk and Gay Head. It was for sailors an evil place and "bad medicine" for Indians, for men who had been wrecked there had been likewise robbed and ill treated—though the honest islanders of today deny it—while the Indians had been driven from their birthright after hundreds of their number had fallen in its defense.

In the winter of 1750-51 the ship Palatine set forth over the seas with thrifty Dutch merchants and emigrants, bound for Philadelphia, with all their goods. A gale delayed them and kept them beating to and fro on the icy seas, unable to reach land. The captain died—it was thought that he was murdered—and the sailors, a brutal set even for those days, threw off all discipline, seized the stores and arms, and starved the passengers into giving up their money.

When those died of hunger whose money had given out—for twenty guilders were demanded for a cup of water and fifty rix dollars for a biscuit—their bodies were flung into the sea, and when the crew had secured all that excited their avarice they took to their boats, leaving ship and passengers to their fate.

It is consoling to know that the sailors never reached a harbor.

The unguided ship, in sight of land, yet tossed at the mercy of every wind and tenanted by walking skeletons, struck off Block Island one calm Sunday morning and the wreckers who lived along the shore set out for her. Their first work was to rescue the passengers; then they returned to strip everything from the hulk that the crew had left; but after getting her in tow a gale sprang up, and seeing that she was doomed to be blown off shore, where she might become a dangerous obstruction or a derelict, they set her on fire. From the rocks they watched her drift into misty darkness, but as the flames mounted to the trucks a scream rang across the whitening sea: a maniac woman had been left on board. The scream was oft repeated, each time more faintly, and the ship passed into the fog and vanished.

A twelvemonth later, on the same evening of the year, the islanders were startled at the sight of a ship in the offing with flames lapping up her sides and rigging, and smoke clouds rolling off before the wind. It burned to the water's edge in sight of hundreds.

In the winter following it came again, and was seen, in fact, for years thereafter at regular intervals, by those who would gladly have forgotten the sight of it (one of the community, an Indian, fell into madness whenever he saw the light), while those who listened caught the sound of a woman's voice raised in agony above the roar of fire and water.

It is interesting to note that Skinner's account of the legend has as the name of the ship *The Palatine*, and the year as 1750-51. Other sources, however, state the year of the wreck as 1738, and the ship as being *The Princess Augusta* (from the Palatinate, a German state of the Holy Roman Empire).

Even more interesting, to the seeker-out of legends, is the following addendum which Skinner placed at the end of his version:

Substantially the same story is told of a point on the North Carolina coast, save that in the latter case the passengers, who were from the Bavarian Palatinate, were put to the knife before their goods were taken. The captain and his crew filled their boats with treasure and pulled away for land, first firing the ship and committing its ghastly freight to the flames. The ship followed them almost to the beach, ere it fell to pieces, as if it were an animate form, bent on vengeance. The pirates landed, but none profited by the crime, all of them dying poor and forsaken.

Are we dealing with two stories here, I wonder? Or just one, but with a confusion of locale?

If more than one story: was it the custom of ships from the Palatinate to feature crews who murdered their passengers? (Speaking of which—the murder of a ship's passengers by its crew—Skinner relates another such tale, which I've taken the liberty to reprint in the next chapter.) 𝄞

THE PHANTOM STEED
(New Shoreham—Block Island—Rhode Island)

If, in these early years of the twenty-first century, travel of any sort, by whatever means, seems fraught with peril, the situation three hundred years ago—as evidenced by the accounts in the preceding chapter—was scarcely better.

In *Myths & Legends of Our Own Land*, Charles M. Skinner includes the following nasty little *conte*. Let it serve as further proof that an eighteenth-century sea voyage was not necessarily conducive to good health.

"THE BUCCANEER"
by
Charles M. Skinner

Among the natives of Block Island was a man named Lee. Born in the last century among fishermen and wreckers, he has naturally taken to the sea for a livelihood, and never having known the influences of education and refinement, he is rude and impetuous in manner.

His ship lies in a Spanish port fitting for sea, but not with freight, for tired of peaceful trading, Lee is equipping his vessel as a privateer. A Spanish lady who has just been bereaved of her husband comes to him to ask a passage to America, for she has no suspicion of his intent. Her jewels and well-filled purse arouse Lee's cupidity, and with pretended sympathy he accedes to her request, even going so far as to allow Señora's favorite horse to be brought aboard.

Hardly is the ship in deep water before the lady's servants are stabbed in their sleep and Lee smashes in the door of her cabin. Realizing his purpose, and preferring to sacrifice life to honor, she eludes him, climbs the rail, and leaps into the sea, while the ship ploughs on. As a poor revenge for being thus balked in his prey the pirate has the beautiful white horse flung overboard, the animal shrilling a neigh that seems to reach to the horizon, and is like nothing ever heard before. But these things he affects to forget in dice and drinking. In a dispute over a division of plunder Lee stabs one of his men and tosses him overboard.

Soon the rovers come to Block Island where, under cover of night, they carry ashore their stealings to hide them in pits and caves, reserving enough gold to buy a welcome from the wreckers, and here they live for a year, gaming and carousing. Their ship has been reported as a pirate and to baffle search it is set adrift.

One night a ruddy star is seen on the sea-verge and the ruffians leave their revelling to look at it, for it is growing into sight fast. It speeds toward them and they can now see that it is a ship—their ship—wrapped in flames.

It stops off shore, and out of the ocean at its prow emerges something white that they say at first is a wave-crest rolling upon the sands; but it does not dissolve as breakers do: it rushes on; it scales the bluff—it is a milk-white horse, that gallops to the men, who inly wonder if this is an alcoholic vision, and glares at Lee. A spell seems to be laid on him, and unable to resist it, the buccaneer mounts the animal.

It rushes away, snorting and plunging, to the highest bluff, whence Lee beholds, in the light of the burning ship, the bodies of all who have been done to death by him, staring into his eyes through the reddening waves.

At dawn the horse sinks under him and he stands there alone. From that hour his companions desert him. They fear to share his curse. He wanders from the island, a broken, miserable man, unwilling to live, afraid to die, refused shelter and friendship, and unable to reach the mainland, for no boat will give him passage.

After a year of this existence the ship returns, the sprectre horse rises from the deep and claims Lee again for a rider. He mounts; the animal speeds away to the cliff but does not pause at the brink this time: with a sickening jump and fall he goes into the sea. Spurning the wave-tops in his flight he makes a circuit of the burning ship, and in the hellish light that fills the air and penetrates to the ocean bottom, the pirate sees again his victims looking up with smiles and arms spread wide to embrace him.

There is a cry of terror as the steed stops short; then a gurgle, and horse and rider have disappeared. The fire ship vanishes and the night is dark. 🏴

BONES THAT RATTLE IN RHODE ISLAND
(North Kingston, Rhode Island)

> *Could there ever be human being*
> *With heart so narrow and small*
> *That never a ghost could hide therein,*
> *To waken at Memory's call?*
> —*Isabella Banks*

Myths & Legends of Our Own Land has proved to be a veritable treasure-trove of forgotten New England ghost stories. I came upon the two-volume work in an obscure used-bookstore-cum-antique shop on Cape Cod. The twin books rested high on a shelf in a dusty, dimly lit corner, where they gave the impression (abetted by the fact that some of the pages had not been "opened," i.e., cut) that this particular two-volume set may have lain there for decades and never been perused by anyone— other than, perhaps, the bookstore's own resident ghosts.

The following story, taken from Volume Two, gives me shivers for a variety of reasons, not least of which is the cavalier treatment

79

of a human skull by the person who chanced upon it.

"THE HEADLESS SKELETON OF SWAMPTOWN"
by
Charles M. Skinner

The boggy portion of North Kingston, Rhode Island, known as Swamptown, is of queer repute in its neighborhood, for Hell Hollow, Pork Hill, Indian Corner, and Kettle Hole have their stories of Indian crimes and witch-meetings.

Here the headless figure of a Negro boy was seen by a belated traveler on a path that leads over the hills. It was a dark night and the figure was revealed in a blaze of blue light. It swayed two and fro for a time, then rose from the ground with a lurch and shot into space, leaving a trail of illumination behind it. Here, too, is Goose-Nest Spring, where the witches dance at night. It dries up every winter and flows through the summer, gushing forth on the same day every year, except once, when a goose took possession of the empty bed and hatched her brood there. That time the water did not flow until she got away with her progeny.

But the most gruesome story of the place is that of the Indian whose skull was found by a road-mender. This unsuspecting person took it home, and as the women would not allow him to carry it into the house, he hung it on a pole outside. Just as the people were starting for bed there came a rattling at the door, and looking out of the windows they saw a skeleton stalking around in quick and angry strides, like those of a person looking for something. But how could that be when the skeleton had neither eyes nor a place to carry them?

It thrashed its bony arms impatiently and its ribs rattled like a xylophone. The spectators were transfixed with fear, all except the culprit, who said through the window in a matter-of-fact way, "I left your head on the pole at the back door."

The skeleton started in that direction, seized the skull, clapped it into the place where a head should have grown on its shoulders, and after shaking its fists in a threatening way at the house, disappeared in the darkness. It is said that he acts as a kind of guard in the neighborhood, to see that none of the other Indians buried there shall be disturbed, as he was.

His principal lounging place is Indian Corner, where there is a rock from which blood flows when the moon shines—a memento, doubtless, of some tragedy that occurred there in times before the white men knew the place. There is iron in the soil, and visitors say that the red color is due to that, and that the spring would flow just as freely on dark nights as on bright one, if any were there to see it, but the natives, who have given some thought to these matters, know better. 🪦

THE GHOST OF HIS FIRST WIFE
(Boston, Brookline, and Northampton, Massachusetts;
and Appledore Island, the Isles of Shoals, Maine)

Why, I have seen thousands of ghosts myself! Many a night, after writing until two o'clock in the morning, and fortifying myself for my work with strong coffee, I have had to shoulder them aside as I went upstairs to bed. —Wilkie Collins, in a conversation with Sidney Dickinson.

Perhaps the rarest of all the many collections of true ghost stories which I possess is a volume of modest proportions titled *True Tales of the Weird*. Its author, Sidney Dickinson, (deceased at the time of publication in 1920) was a journalist and lecturer and had been correspondent for a number of newspapers and magazines, among them the New York *Times*, *Scribner's Monthly*, the Boston *Journal*, and the Springfield *Republican*.

Roughly two-thirds of the book is Dickinson's account of his personal involvement in a series of hauntings in Australia, associated with a notorious murderer whose trial and execution

Dickinson attended—and is well worth the reading. The first four chapters, however, deal with hauntings closer to home; they fit in nicely with *this* book's theme of New England ghosts.

Of all the gleanings from the archives which I've rescued and dusted off for inclusion in *The Haunted Pram*, the stories from *True Tales of the Weird* seem to lend themselves the most to credence. As the author himself stated, "These stories are not 'founded upon fact;' they *are* fact." In a "Prefatory Note," Gertrude Ogden Tubby (I just love the sound of that name!), an official with the American Society for Psychical Research, wrote: "It is a pleasure to testify that the manuscript has been submitted with abundant testimonies from the individuals who knew their author at first hand . . . These accounts bear internal evidence to their true psychic origin . . . They ring true. And they are, in addition, moving human documents, with a strong literary appeal."

I hereby present the four interrelated stories, in a much abridged format, and interspersed with my own notes and comments.

"A Mystery of Two Continents"
by
Sydney Dickinson

Some years ago, in the course of a tour of art study which took me through the principal countries of Europe, I found myself in Naples. The time of year was late February and the season, even for Southern Italy, was much advanced. In visiting the Island of Capri I found this most charming spot in the Vesuvian

Bay smiling and verdant, and was tempted by the brilliant sunshine and warm breezes to explore the hilly country which rose behind the port.

The fields upon the heights were green with grass and spangled with delicate white flowers bearing a yellow center, which while smaller than our familiar American field-daisies, and held upon more slender stalks, reminded me of them. Having in mind certain friends in then bleak New England, I plucked a number of these blossoms and placed them between the leaves of my guidebook—Baedeker's "Southern Italy"—intending to enclose them in letters which I planned to write.

Returning to Naples, the many interests of that city put out of my head for the time the thought of letter-writing, and three days later I took the train to Rome, with my correspondence still in arrears. The first day of my stay in Rome was devoted to an excursion by carriage into the Campagna, and on the way back to the city I stopped to see the Tomb of Cecilia Metella, a beautiful memorial with its massive walls, its roof (now fallen and leaving the sepulcher open to the sky), and heavy turf which covers the earth of its interior. This green carpet of Nature, when I visited the tomb, was thickly strewn with fragrant violets, and of these, as of the daisy-like flowers I had found in Capri, I collected several, and placed them in my guidebook—this time Baedeker's "Central Italy."

The next day, calling at my bankers', I saw an announcement that letters posted before four o'clock that afternoon would be forwarded to catch the mail for New York by a specially fast steamer. I hastened back to my hotel. The most important duty of the moment seemed to be the writing of a letter to my wife, then living in Boston, and to this I particularly addressed myself.

I concluded my letter as follows: "In Naples I found February to be like our New England May, and in Capri I found the heights of the island spangled over with delicate flowers, some of which I plucked and enclose in this letter. I send you also some violets which I gathered yesterday at the Tomb of Cecilia Metella, outside of Rome.

Having finished the letter, I took from the guide-book on "Central Italy" the violets from the Tomb of Cecilia Metella, enclosed them with the sheets I had written in an envelope, sealed and addressed it, and was about to affix the stamp, when it suddenly occurred to me that I had left out the flowers I had plucked at Capri. These, I recalled, were still in the other guide-book, which I had laid away in my portmanteau.

Accordingly I unstrapped and unlocked the portmanteau, found the guide-book, took out the flowers, opened and destroyed the envelope already addressed, added the daisies to the violets, and put the whole into a new enclosure, which I duly dropped into the mail-box at the bankers'.

During my year abroad my wife was living, as I have said, in Boston, occupying at the Winthrop House, on Bowdoin Street— a hotel which has since, I believe, been taken down—a suite of rooms comprising parlor, bedroom, and bath. With her was my daughter by a former marriage, whose mother had died at her birth, some seven years before. On the same floor were apartments occupied by Mrs. Celia Thaxter, a woman whose name is well known in American literature, and with whom my wife sustained a very intimate friendship.

About ten days after I had posted my letter, enclosing the flowers from Capri and Rome, my wife suddenly awoke in the middle of the night, and saw standing at the foot of the bed the form of the child's mother. The aspect of the apparition was so serene and gracious that, although greatly startled, she felt no alarm. Then she heard, as if from a voice at a great distance, these words: "I have brought you some flowers from Sidney." At the next instant the figure vanished.

The visitation had been so brief that my wife, although she at once arose and lighted the gas, argued with herself that she had been dreaming, and after a few minutes extinguished the light and returned to bed, where she slept soundly until six o'clock the next morning. Always an early riser, she dressed at once and went from her bedroom, where the child was still sleeping, to her parlor.

In the center of the room was a table, covered with a green cloth, and as she entered and happened to glance at it she saw, to her surprise, a number of dried flowers scattered over it. A part of these she recognized as violets, but the rest were unfamiliar to her, although they resembled very small daisies.

After examining these strange blossoms for a time she returned to her chamber and awakened the child, whom she then took to see the flowers, and asked her if she knew anything about them.

"Why, no, mamma," the little girl replied. "I have never seen them before."

So the flowers were gathered up and placed on the shelf above the fireplace, and during the morning were exhibited to Mrs. Thaxter, who came in for a chat, and who, like my wife, could make nothing of the matter.

At about four o'clock in the afternoon the postman called bearing several letters. Among them was one that was postmarked "Rome" and addressed in my handwriting, and with this she sat down as the first to be read. It contained an account, among other things, of my experiences in Naples and Rome, and in due course mentioned the enclosure of flowers. There were, however, no flowers whatever in the letter, although each sheet and the envelope were carefully examined; my wife even shook her skirts and made a search upon the carpet, thinking that the flowers might have fallen out as the letter was opened.

Nothing could be found—yet ten hours before the arrival of the letter, flowers exactly such as it described had been found on the center table.

According to *The Oxford Companion to American Literature, Fourth Edition*, Celia Thaxter— "a woman whose name is well known in American literature"—was born in 1835 and died in 1894. She was the daughter of a lighthouse keeper on the Isles of Shoals (which, incidentally, figure as the locales in several of the stories which follow) off the coasts of New Hampshire and Maine, and spent most of her life there.

She drew upon the islands and the surrounding sea for inspiration for her poetry and prose, and was acquainted with such famous writers as Thoreau, Lowell, and Whittier.

According to A. Hyatt Verrill (*Along New England Shores*), Appledore Island was owned by Celia Thaxter's father, the Honorable Thomas B. Leighton, who built a popular summer hotel (site of the second Mrs. Dickinson's vision of "The Midnight Horseman," recounted later in this chapter.) Both Thaxter and her father are buried on the island.

Van Wyck Brooks—in *New England: Indian Summer 1865-1915*—devotes several pages to Celia Thaxter. He mentions that she—along with many other prominent New England writers of her day—was interested in spiritualism and on occasion acted as a medium during seances. Her own life would, it occurs to me, provide the basis for an interesting ghost story. "Her father, the lighthouse-keeper, who had been disappointed in his youth, had vowed he would never set foot on the mainland again." Celia herself never saw a town from the age of five until the age of sixteen. "Her only companions," Brooks tells us, "were the goats that browsed by the little stone cottage." And she "ranged over the ridges and gorges, haunted with the tales of ghosts and pirates . . ."

One of these tales concerned "'Old Bob,' the ghost, with the ring about his neck and the face that was pale and dreadful." Old Bob, it seems, got around. And still does, if not on the Isles of Shoals, at least in books about the Isles. We'll encounter him again, below, in the chapter titled "Her Golden Hair Unbound," and again in "These Haunted Isles."

"A Spirit of Health"
by
Sidney Dickinson

It is now thirty-one years ago that the wife of my youth, after less than a year of married life, was taken from me by death, leaving to me an infant daughter, in whom all the personal and mental traits of the mother gradually reproduced themselves in a remarkable degree. Some three years later I married again, and the child, who during that period had been in the care of her grandparents, was taken into the newly-formed home.

A strong affection between the new mother and the little girl was established at once, and their relations soon became more like those of blood than of adoption.

At the time in which these events occurred I was traveling in Europe, and my wife and daughter were living in Boston. In the adjoining town of Brookline there resided a lady of wealth and social prominence, Mrs. John W. Candler. She was a woman of rare beauty and possessed unusual intellectual gifts; she was also a close personal friend of Mrs. Thaxter. It often happened that Mrs. Thaxter, and my wife and child, were guests for considerable periods at her luxurious residence.

One afternoon in mid-winter, Mrs. Candler drove into the city to call upon my wife, and finding her suffering from a somewhat obstinate cold, urged her, with her usual warmth and heartiness, to return home with her for a couple of days, for the sake of the comforts which her house could afford as compared with those of the hotel. My wife demurred to this, chiefly on the

89

ground that, as the weather was very severe, she did not like to take the child with her, since being rather delicate that winter although not actually ill, she dared not remove her, even temporarily, from the equable temperature of the hotel.

While the matter was being discussed another caller was announced in the person of Miss Mae Harris Anson, a young woman of some eighteen years, who was pursuing a course of study at the New England Conservatory of Music. Miss Anson was very fond of children, and possessed an unusual talent for entertaining them—and thus was a great favorite of my little daughter. Mrs. Candler suggested that Miss Anson might be willing to care for the child during my wife's absence. Miss Anson at once assented, saying that she would like nothing better than to exchange her boardinghouse for a hotel for awhile.

The next morning she arrived at the hotel prepared for a two or three days' stay, and that afternoon my wife was driven by sleigh to Mrs. Candler's home.

The afternoon and evening passed without incident, and my wife retired early to bed, being assigned a room next to Mrs. Candler, and one that could be entered only through that lady's apartment. The next morning she arose rather late, and yielding to the arguments of her hostess, who insisted that she should not undergo the exertion of going down to breakfast, that repast was served in her room, and she partook of it while seated in an easy chair at a table before an open fire that blazed cheerily in the wide chimney-place. The meal finished and the table removed, she continued to sit for some time in her comfortable chair, being attired only in dressing-gown and slippers, considering whether she should go to bed again, as Mrs. Candler had recommended, or prepare herself to rejoin her friend, whom she could hear talking in the adjoining room with another member of the household.

The room in which she was sitting had a large window fronting upon the southwest, and the morning sun, shining from a cloudless

90

sky, poured through it a flood of light that stretched nearly to her feet, and formed a golden track upon the carpet. Her eyes wandered from one to another object in the luxurious apartment, and as they returned from one of these excursions to a regard of her more immediate surroundings, she was startled to perceive that someone was with her—one who, standing in full light that came through the window, was silently observing her.

Some subtle and unclassified sense informed her that the figure in the sunlight was not of mortal mold—it was indistinct in form and outline, and seemed to be a part of, rather than separate from, the radiance that surrounded it. It was the figure of a young and beautiful woman with golden hair and blue eyes, and from both face and eyes was carried the impression of a great anxiety; a robe of some filmy white material covered her from neck to feet, and bare arms, extending from flowing sleeves, were stretched forth in a gesture of appeal.

My wife, stricken with a feeling in which awe dominated fear, lay back in her chair for some moments silently regarding the apparition, not knowing if she were awake or dreaming. A strange familiarity in the face troubled her, for she knew she had never seen it before—then understanding came to her, and the recollection of photographs, and of the features of her daughter by adoption, flashed upon her mind the instant conviction that she was gazing at the mother who died when the child was born.

"What is it?" she finally found strength to whisper. "Why do you come to me?"

The countenance of the apparition took on an expression of trouble more acute even than before.

"The child!" The cry came from the shadowy lips distinctly, yet as if uttered at a great distance. "Go back to town at once!"

"But why?" my wife inquired.

The figure began to fade away, as if reabsorbed in the light that enveloped it. "Go to your room and look in your bureau

91

drawer!" And only the sunlight was to be seen in the spot where the phantom had stood.

For some moments my wife remained reclining in her chair, completely overcome by her strange vision; then she got upon her feet and half ran, half staggered, into the next room where Mrs. Candler and her companion were still conversing.

"Something terrible is happening in town! Please, please take me to my rooms at once!" And she hurriedly related what she had seen.

Mrs. Candler endeavored to soothe her—she had been dreaming; all must be well with the child, otherwise Miss Anson would at once inform them. Moreover, rather than have her brave a ride to town in the bitter cold, she would send a servant after luncheon to inquire for news at the hotel.

My wife was not convinced by these arguments but finally yielded to them; Mrs. Candler gave her the morning paper as a medium for quieting her mind, and she returned with it to her room and resumed her seat in the easy chair.

She had hardly begun her reading, however, when the newspaper was snatched from her hand and thrown to the opposite side of the room, and as she started up in alarm she saw the apparition again standing in the sunlight, and again heard the voice—this time in a tone of imperious command: "Go to your rooms at once and look in your bureau drawer!"

At the utterance of these words the apparition vanished, leaving my wife so overwhelmed that for some time she was powerless to move. Then reason returned to her, and she was able to regain her friend's room and acquaint her with the facts of this second visitation. This time Mrs. Candler made no attempt to oppose her. The horses and sleigh were ordered from the stables, and in half an hour both ladies were speeding toward Boston.

When they reached the entrance of the hotel my wife sprang from the sleigh and rushed upstairs, with Mrs. Candler close behind her, burst into the door of her rooms like a whirlwind, and discovered—the child absorbed in architectural pursuits with a set of building blocks in the middle of the sitting room, and Miss Anson calmly reading a novel in a rocking chair by the window!

Mrs. Candler at once burst out laughing; my wife's face showed intense bewilderment—then, crying, "She said 'look in the bureau drawer!'" she hurried into the bedroom with Mrs. Candler at her heels.

The bureau, which stood at the head of the child's bed, presented an entirely innocent appearance; nevertheless my wife went straight up to it, and firmly grasping the handles, pulled out the topmost drawer. Instantly a mass of flame burst forth, accompanied by a cloud of acrid smoke that billowed to the ceiling, and the whole interior of the bureau seemed to be ablaze.

Mrs. Candler seized a pitcher of water and dashed it upon the fire, and Miss Anson flew into the hall, arousing the house with her cries. Mrs. Thaxter, who was at the moment coming into my wife's apartment, hurried in, saw the blazing bureau, and turned quickly to summon help. Employees came running with an extinguisher, and in five minutes the danger was over.

My wife, who was a skillful painter in oils, was accustomed to keep her colors and brushes in the upper drawer of the bureau. She had also, and very carelessly, placed in a corner of the drawer a quantity of loose rags which had become thoroughly saturated with oil and turpentine from cleaning her palette and brushes. Some time before, she had put a whole package of matches into a stewpan, in which she heated water, and set the pan with these paints and rags. Then, one night when in a hurry for some hot water, she had gone in, in the dark, and forgetting all about the matches had dumped them upon the tubes of oil paints. Spontaneous combustion was the eventual result.

93

"THE MIRACLE OF THE FLOWERS"
by
Sidney Dickinson

Some months after the happenings recorded in the two previous narratives, I was spending the summer following my return from Europe in Northampton, Massachusetts, at the residence of my father, having with me my wife and child. The mother of the child was a resident of the town at the time of our marriage, and her body reposed in our family's lot in the cemetery.

The little girl was passionately fond of flowers, and her indulgent grandfather had that summer allotted to her sole use a plot six feet square in his spacious gardens, which became the pride of her heart from the brilliant array of blooms which she had coaxed to grow in it. Her favorite flowers were pansies, with the seeds of which she had planted nearly one-half of the space. They had germinated successfully and flourished, and formed a solid mass, with every conceivable variety.

One afternoon my wife and I set out for a walk through the meadows that stretched away from the back of the grounds, and on our return some two hours later we saw at a distance the child standing upon the terrace awaiting us, bearing a large bouquet of her favorite pansies in her hand. She ran to meet us and extended the pansies to my wife, saying, "Mamma, I picked them for you from my pansy-bed."

My wife thanked the child and kissed her, and we went upstairs to our room to prepare for supper. I placed the bunch of pansies in a vase with water. After supper my wife and I called upon some relatives who lived about a quarter of a mile away. We spent a pleasant evening with them, leaving on our return at ten o'clock.

The night was warm and perfectly calm, and as there was no moon, the way was dark save where, here and there, a street lamp threw about its little circle of light. As we turned into the street

94

which led to my father's house we passed under a row of maple trees whose heavy foliage made the darkness even more profound, and beside a high hedge which enclosed the spacious grounds of a mansion that stood at the corner of the two highways. This hedge extended for a distance of about fifty yards. We were at a point about midway of the hedge when my wife , who was the nearer to it, suddenly stopped and exclaimed: "Was it you that gave that pull at my shawl?" and readjusted the garment—a light fleecy affair—which was half off her left shoulder.

"Why, no," I replied. "What do you mean?"

"I mean," she answered, "that I felt a hand seize my shawl and try to draw it away from me."

I suggested that it might have caught upon a twig. She insisted, however, that some person had laid a hand upon her. We went on and had left the hedge behind, and were within a few feet of a street lamp, when my wife stopped a second time, declaring that her shawl had been seized again. Sure enough, the garment was as before, lying half off her shoulder, and this time obviously not from any projecting twig.

On a sudden my wife seized my arm with a convulsive grip, and raising her eyes whispered: "Did you see *that?*"

I followed the direction of her gaze, but could see nothing, and told her so, in the same breath asking her what she meant.

"It is Minnie!" she gasped—thus uttering the name of my dead wife. "She has her hands full of flowers! Oh, Minnie, Minnie, what are you doing?" She hid her face in her hands.

I clasped her in my arms, thinking she was about to faint, and gazed fearfully above us. At the same time I felt a shower of soft objects strike upon my upturned face, and saw against the light what seemed like blossoms floating to the ground.

As soon as I could quiet my wife I made a search of the ground. The objects whose fall I had both felt and seen were plainly evident, even in the dim light, and I gathered up a number of them and carried them under the lamp. They were pansies, freshly gathered, and with their leaves and stems damp, as if just taken from water.

Hastening to the house, we went directly to our room, and lighting the gas looked eagerly toward the shelf where we had left the vase filled with pansies some three hours before. The vase was there, half-filled with water, but not a single flower was standing in it.

A second episode occurred the following winter. Business took me from Boston, and during my absence my wife and daughter were invited by Mrs. Candler to spend a few days at her house in Brookline.

On the second day of their visit the child became suddenly ill, and as evening drew on exhibited rather alarming symptoms of fever. A physician was summoned who prescribed remedies, and directed that the patient should be put to bed at once. This was done, and at about ten o'clock my wife, accompanied by Mrs. Candler and several other ladies who were also guests, went quietly upstairs to observe her condition before retiring for the night themselves.

The upper floor was reached by a very broad staircase which branched near the top to give access to the chambers upon a wide hall. The room in which the child lay was about halfway around this hall on the left-hand side. The ladies entered the chamber and the hostess turned up the gas, showing the child peacefully slumbering and with forehead and hands moist with perspiration. As the night was a bitter cold one in mid-January, the mistress suggested that additional covering should be placed upon the bed, and produced from another room an eider-down counterpane, covered with scarlet silk, which was carefully arranged without awakening the sleeper.

96

All then left the room and started downstairs again, the hostess being the last to go out, after lowering the gas until it showed only a point of light. They were near the bottom of the staircase when my wife suddenly cried out: "Oh, there is Minnie! She passed by me up the stairs, and has gone into the room. Oh, I know something dreadful is going to happen!"

She rushed frantically to the upper floor, followed by the others in a body. At the half-open door of the child's room they all stopped and listened, but no sound came from within. Then, mustering up courage and clinging to each others' hands, they went softly in, and Mrs. Candler turned up the gas. Half blinded by the sudden glare of the gaslight, they could not for a moment credit what their eyes showed them: that the sleeping child lay under a coverlet, not of scarlet as they had left her scarcely a minute before, but of snowy white. The scarlet eider-down counterpane was completely covered with pure white lilies on long stalks, so spread about and lying in such quantities that the surface of the bed was hidden under their bloom.

By actual count there were more than two hundred of these rich and beautiful blossoms strewn upon the coverlet, representing a moderate fortune at that time of year, and probably unprocurable though all the conservatories in the city had been searched for them. They were carefully gathered and placed about the house in vases, jugs, and every other receptacle that could be pressed into service to hold them, filling the room for several days with their fragrance until, like other flowers, they faded and died.

In the final story borrowed from *True Tales of the Weird* the ghost of Sidney's first wife takes a leave of absence. But his second wife remains very much present and percipient. In "The Haunted Bungalow," the detailed account of ghostly occurrences in Australia which constitutes the last two-thirds of the book,

Sidney says of her: "She who was throughout her life more sensitive than most of us to occult forces that at times appear to be in operation about us, has since crossed the frontier of the Undiscovered Country, there to find, perhaps, solution to some of the riddles that have perplexed both her and me. Intensely human as she was, and in all things womanly, her susceptibility to weird and uncomprehended influences must always seem a contradiction—and the more so since they always came upon her not only without invitation, but even in opposition to a will of unusual force and sanity."

"THE MIDNIGHT HORSEMAN"
by
Sidney Dickinson

On a brilliant moonlit evening in August, 1885, a considerable party of friends and more or less intimate acquaintances of the hostess assembled at the summer cottage of Mrs. Thaxter at Appledore Island, Isles of Shoals.

[Dickinson goes on to describe at length the charms of the "cottage" and the conversation of the distinguished guests. All this leads up to the moment, late in the evening, when his wife experiences a sudden vision.]

My wife suddenly exclaimed: "How strange! Why, the wall of the room seems to have been removed, and I can see rocks and the sea, and the moonlight shining upon them!

"It is growing stranger still. I do not see the sea any more. I see a long, straight road, with great trees like elms here and there on the side of it, and casting dark shadows across it. There is a man standing in the middle of the road, in the shadow of one of the trees. Now he is coming toward me and I can see his face in the moonlight. Why! it is John Weiss!" (naming the Liberal clergyman and writer whom most of us had known in Boston, and who had died some five or six years before). What are you doing here, and what does this mean? He smiles, but does not speak. Now he has turned and gone back into the shadow of the tree again.

"Now I can see something coming along the road some distance away. A man on horseback. He is riding slowly, and he has his head bent and slouch hat over his eyes, so that I cannot see his face. Now John Weiss steps out of the shadow into the moonlight; the horse sees him and stops; he rears up in the air and whirls about and begins to run back in the direction from which he came. The man on his back pulls him up, lashes him with his whip, turns him around, and tries to make him go forward. The horse is terrified and backs again, trying to break away from his rider. The man strikes him again, but he will not advance.

"The man dismounts and tries to lead the horse, looking about to see what he is frightened at. I can see his face very clearly—I should know him anywhere! John Weiss is walking toward him, but the man does not see him. The horse does, though, and plunges and struggles, but the man is strong and holds him fast. Now John Weiss is so close to the man that he sees him, and is horribly frightened. He steps back but John Weiss does not follow—only points his hand at him. The man jumps on his horse and beats him fiercely with his whip, and the two fly back down the road and disappear in the distance."

We were all profoundly impressed by this graphic recital and spent some time discussing what possible meaning the strange vision could have; but we were compelled to abandon all efforts to elucidate it, and it was not until seven months later that the sequel to the mystery was furnished.

Early in March of the following year a party of eight or ten persons was dining at the house of Mrs. Candler, in Brookline.

[Once again Dickinson describes at considerable length the evening's activities leading up to the events that follow.]

Directly facing the open door, and the only one of the company so seated, was my wife—who suddenly startled us all by springing to her feet and crying out: "There he is! The man I saw at the Isles of Shoals last summer!"

"What is it?" I inquired. "An apparition?"

"No," she exclaimed. "A living man. I saw him look around the edge of the door and immediately draw back again. He is here to rob the house!" She rushed out into the hall with the whole company in pursuit. The servants, who by this time had gone to bed, were aroused and set to work to examine the lower floors, while we above searched every room, but in each case without result.

As I passed through a large apartment some thirty feet long by twenty wide, which was used for dancing parties, I felt a current of cold air, which I immediately traced, by the swaying of one of the heavy curtains, to a window with its folds covered. Going up to the drapery and drawing it aside, I saw that the window was half open. Further investigation showed, by tell-tale marks in the snow, the footsteps of a man running with long strides through the grounds to the street, two hundred yards away, where they were lost in the confused tracks of the public highway. From that time to the present the mystery has remained unsolved. ₿

THE OLD, PALE TERROR
(Plymouth, Massachusetts)

foxfire: A phosphorescent glow, especially that produced by certain fungi found on rotting wood —The American Heritage Dictionary of the English Language

> *We easily discount the petty superstitions that tradition and the frills of literature have made for us. That that grows out of the foxfire in the swamp has its roots too far back in the inheritance of the race to be discounted. The cemetery ghosts make only a friendly illumination for the last stages of a pleasant trip. —* Winthrop Packard

Some thirty-five or forty years ago, while fossicking through the cluttered tables of a flea market in Norton, Massachusetts, I stumbled upon what has proved to be a veritable treasure-trove of New-Englandiana, a copy of Winthrop Packard's *Old Plymouth Trails*. At the time—despite my callow youth—I was delighted with the find; I even remember the price I paid for the book, which though lacking a dust jacket (and after repeated readings) remains in excellent condition: four dollars. Four dollars for a book of inestimable worth!

Purists may object that the excerpt which follows is not, in the literal sense, a ghost story. Ah, but . . .

"GHOSTS OF THE NORTHEASTER"
by
Winthrop Packard

More years ago than I like to count, there used to come to my town an old man with a magic lantern. He would hire the audience room in the ancient town hall for an evening, hang up a sheet, charge ten cents admission and show to a crowd of wondering and delighted urchins pictures wonderful, humorous and startling. He always wound up with one for which he apologized, then showed it with much gusto, saying that he did not believe in such things himself, but that some people liked to see them. This was "death on the pale horse," and boys used to band together and see one another home through the darkness after looking at it.

The creature that pointed his fleshless arm at me from the thicket was not that of the old time magic lantern exhibit, but it reminded me of that immediately, probably because it struck the same formless shudder through my bones. Yet it was only for a moment.

I had seen such phosphorescent ghosts before, and I had but to step boldly forward and give the stub a kick to send the specter flying in fragments that dropped like huge glowworms in chunks to the sodden ground. Often in a northeast rain after long drought a rotten birch stump will thus glow with phosphorescent fire producing a most formidable and tradition-satisfying ghost.

There is nothing to be feared in a phosphorescent birch stub, even with the drip of rain from the leaves making stealthy, ghostly footfalls all through the wood and the voice of the east wind in the trees overhead beginning to take up a querulous, wordless complaint that moved back and forth with the footfalls. Foxfire is a common enough phenomenon. It is easy to explain it all as I do now. The strange part of such things is always that, at the time, no matter what a man's training and experience, he feels creeping back and forth in his bones the old, pale terror of primitive man. ᚴ

HER GOLDEN HAIR UNBOUND
(White Island, Isles of Shoals, New Hampshire)

With a total area of barely six hundred acres, the Isles of Shoals are about the most desolate, barren and forbidding real estate in all of New England —A. Hyatt Verrill, Along New England Shores

In the fascinating and informative book about the history and folklore of the New England coastline from which the epigraph above is taken, A. Hyatt Verrill recounts a chilling incident from King Philip's War that took place on Star Island.

While the men of the island were off fishing, the Indians raided it. To escape certain death, Betty Moody grabbed her children and hid with them in the fissures of a rock. The shouts of the savages and the screams of her neighbors frightened the children, and one of them began to cry. To silence the child she strangled it. Alas, to no avail. The warriors discovered her hiding place. To avoid capture, and remorseful for what she had done, Betty clasped the other child in her arms and flung herself into the sea.

In *Shapes That Haunt New England* I used the tragic story of Betty Moody as the basis for a fictional ghost story of my own. But there are any number of actual ghosts connected with the islands. For instance, Verrill writes about "the ghostly woman of White Island." A more detailed version of the story appears below:

"THE WATCHER ON WHITE ISLAND"
by
Charles M. Skinner

The Isles of Shoals, a little archipelago of wind- and wave-swept rocks that may be seen on clear days from the New Hampshire coast, have been the scene of some mishaps and some crimes. On Boone Island, where the Nottingham galley went down one hundred and fifty years ago, the survivors turned cannibals to escape starvation, while Haley's Island is peopled by shipwrecked Spanish ghosts that hail vessels and beg for passage back to their country.

The pirate Teach, or Blackbeard, used to put in at these islands to hide his treasure, and one of his lieutenants spent some time on White Island with a beautiful girl whom he had abducted from her home in Scotland and who, in spite of his rough life, had learned to love him.

It was while walking with her on this rock, forgetful of his trade and the crimes he had been stained with, that one of his men ran up to report a sail that was standing toward the islands. The pirate ship was quickly prepared for action, but before embarking, mindful of possible flight or captivity, the lieutenant made his mistress swear that she would guard the buried treasure if it should be till doomsday.

The ship he was hurrying to meet came smoothly on until the

pirate craft was well in range, when ports flew open along the stranger's sides, guns were run out, and a heavy broadside splintered through the planks of the robber galley. It was a man-of-war, not a merchantman, that had run Blackbeard down.

The war-ship closed and grappled with the corsair, but while the sailors were standing at the chains ready to leap aboard and complete the subjugation of the outlaws a mass of flame burst from the pirate ship, both vessels were hurled in fragments through the air, and a roar went for miles along the sea. Blackbeard's lieutenant had fired the magazine rather than submit to capture, and had blown the two ships into a common ruin.

A few of both crews floated to the islands on planks, sore from burns and bruises, but none survived the cold and hunger of the winter. The pirate's mistress was the first to die; still, true to her promise, she keeps her watch, and at night is dimly seen on a rocky point gazing toward the east, her tall figure enveloped in a cloak, her golden hair unbound upon her shoulders, her pale face still as marble.

According to Celia Thaxter in *Among the Isles of Shoals*—a diminutive volume which, since its publication in 1873, has become a minor (if somewhat neglected) classic—our lady of the golden hair led an active, shall we say . . . *after*life. Thaxter's account (which I've shortened a bit) follows:

from AMONG THE ISLES OF SHOALS
by
Celia Thaxter

I have before me a weird, romantic legend of these islands, in a time-stained, battered newspaper of forty years ago. I regret that it is too long to be given entire, for the unknown writer tells his story well. He came to the Shoals for the benefit of his failing health, and remained there late into the autumn of 1826, "in the family of a wealthy fisherman."

He tells his strange story in this way: "It was one of those awfully still mornings which cloud-gazers will remember as characterizing the autumn months." He stood on a low, long point fronting the east, with the cliffs behind him, gazing out upon the calm, when suddenly he became aware of a figure standing near him. It was a woman wrapped closely in a dark sea-cloak, with a profusion of light hair flowing loosely over her shoulders.

Fair as a lily and as still, she stood with her eyes fixed on the far distance, without a motion, without a sound. "Thinking her one of the inhabitants of a neighboring island who was watching for the return of a fishing-boat, or perhaps a lover, I did not immediately address her; but seeing no appearance of any vessel, at length accosted her with, 'Well, my pretty maiden, do you see anything of him?'

"She turned instantly, and fixing on me the largest and most melancholy blue eyes I ever beheld, said quietly, 'He *will* come again.'" Then she disappeared round a jutting rock and left him marveling, and though he had come to the island for a forenoon's stroll, he was desirous to get back to Star and his own quarters.

Fairly at home again, he was inclined to look upon his adventure as a dream, a mere delusion arising from his illness, but concluded to seek in his surroundings something to substantiate, or remove the idea. Finding nothing—no woman on the island resembling the one he had met—he resolved to go again to the same spot.

This time it blew half a gale; the fishermen in vain endeavored to dissuade him. He was so intensely anxious to be assured of the truth or fiction of the impression of the day before that he could not refrain, and launched his boat, "which sprang strongly upon

108

the whitened waters," and unfurling his one sail, he rounded a point and was soon safely sheltered in a small cove on the leeward side.

Then he leaped the chasms and made his way to the scene of his bewilderment. The sea was rolling over the low point; the spot where he had stood the day before "was a chaos of tumult, yet even then I could have sworn I heard with the same deep distinctness the quiet words of the maiden, 'He *will* come again,' and then a low, remotely-ringing laugher. All the latent superstition of my nature rose up over me, overwhelming as the waves upon the rocks."

After that, day after day, when the weather would permit, he visited the desolate place, to find the golden-haired ghost, and often she stood beside him, "silent as when I first saw her, except to say, as then, 'He *will* come again,' and these words came upon the mind rather than upon the ear.

"I observed that the shells never crashed beneath her footsteps, nor did her garments rustle. In the bright, awful calm of noon and in the rush of the storm there was the same heavy stillness over her. When the winds were so furious that I could scarcely stand in their sweep, the light hair lay upon the forehead of the maiden without lifting a fiber. Her great blue eyeballs never moved in their sockets, and always shone with the same fixed, unearthly gleam. The motion of her person was imperceptible; I knew that she was here, and that she was gone."

So sweet a ghost was hardly a salutary influence in the life of our invalid. She "held him with her glittering eye" till he grew quite beside himself. "The last time I stood with her, was just at the evening of a tranquil day. It was a lovely sunset. A few gold-edged clouds crowned the hills of the distant continent, and the sun had gone down behind them. The ocean lay blushing beneath the blushes of the sky, and even the ancient rocks seemed smiling in the glance of the departing day.

109

"Peace, deep peace was the pervading power. The waters, lapsing among the caverns, spoke of it, and it was visible in the silent motion of the small boats, which loosening their white sails in the cove of Star Island, passed slowly out, one by one to the night-fishing." In the glow of sunset he fancied the ghost grew rosy and human. In the mellow light her cold eyes seemed to soften. But he became suddenly so overpowered with terror that 'kneeling in shuddering fearfulness, he swore never more to look upon that spot, and never did again."

Going back to Star he met his old fisherman, who without noticing his agitation, told him quietly that he knew where he had been and what he had seen; that he himself had seen her.

Would I had met this lily-fair ghost! Is it she, I wonder, who laments like a Banshee before the tempests, wailing through the gorges, "He will *not* come again"? Perhaps it was she who frightened a merry party of people at Duck Island, whither they had betaken themselves for a day's pleasure a few summers ago. In the center of the low island stood a deserted shanty which some strange fisherman had built there several years before, and left empty, tenanted only by the mournful winds. It was blown down the September following. It was a rude hut with two rough rooms and one square window, or rather opening for a window, for sash or glass there was none.

One of our party proposed going to look after the boats, as the breeze freshened and blew directly upon the cove where we had landed. We were gathered on the eastern end of the island when he returned, and kneeling on the withered grass where we were grouped, he said suddenly, "Coming back from the boats, I faced the fish-house, and as I neared it I saw someone watching me from the window. I thought it was one of you. But when I was near enough to have recognized it, I perceived it to be the strange countenance of a woman, wan as death; a face young, yet with a look in it of infinite age. Old! It was older than the Sphinx in the desert!

110

"It looked as if it had been watching and waiting for me since the beginning of time. I walked straight into the hut. There wasn't a vestige of a human being there; it was absolutely empty."

All the warmth and brightness of the summer day could hardly prevent a chill from creeping into our veins as we listened to this calmly delivered statement, and we actually sent a boat back to Appledore for a large yacht to take us home, for the wind rose fast and "gurly grew the sea," and we half expected the wan woman would come and carry our companion off bodily before our eyes.

White Island is not the only spot on the Isles of Shoals haunted by a ghost whose sole purpose in life (uh, better correct that to *after*life) appears to be the guarding of buried treasure. On Appledore, Verrill tells us, "the ghost of a long-dead pirate" was so often seen that the inhabitants regarded him as a member of the community and referred to him as "Old Bab." In addition to being a rather frightening specter "with a villainous face" and "snaky, greasy hair and whiskers," Old Bab was distinguished by a "scrawny neck scarred by the mark of a hangman's rope."

Readers who are interested in learning more about the various spooks and phantoms of these islands—including "Old Bab" (or Philip Babb, which apparently was his proper appellation) and "the pirate bride"—are referred to *Maine Ghosts and Legends: 26 Encounters with the Supernatural* by Thomas A. Verde.

Among many interests, Celia Thaxter enjoyed the art of gardening. *An Island Garden*, her classic account of the recreation of an English cottage garden on the Isles of Shoals, originally appeared in 1894 and has been brought back in a facsimile edition by Houghton Mifflin, its original publisher

In the "Gosh, it's a small world!" department, guess who I met the other day? Why, none other than Celia Thaxter. No, not her *ghost*, but Celia in the flesh. Well actually it was a woman impersonating Celia Thaxter at the New England Spring Flower Show in Boston. One of the displays at the show was a recreation of Thaxter's island garden; a talented garden designer named Maryann Burr, appropriately dressed in Victorian garb, assumed the role of Celia Thaxter and graciously greeted visitors, just as Mrs. Thaxter herself must have a century and a half ago.

As I said, it was not Celia Thaxter's ghost that I encountered— but meeting her while researching this book is an eerie coincidence nonetheless, wouldn't you say? 🪦

THE WILD MAN OF WELLFLEET
(Wellfleet, Massachusetts)

Could there ever be man or woman
So lonely and loveless through life,
Was never haunted by kith or kin,
Spirit of peace or strife?
—Isabella Banks

Pirates are—almost by definition—cruel, violent, ruthless, and evil. Is it any wonder then that they are so often the subject of grisly ghost stories? The following brief history of one lone pirate is, for the most part, unremarkable . . . except for that last sentence.

"THE WILD MAN OF CAPE COD"
by
Charles M. Skinner

For years after Bellamy's pirate ship was wrecked at Wellfleet, by false pilotage on the part of one of his captives, a strange-looking man used to travel up and down the Cape, who was believed to be one of the few survivors of that night of storm, and of the hanging that others underwent after getting ashore.

The pirates had money when the ship struck; it was found in the pockets of a hundred drowned who were cast on the beach, as well as among the sands of the Cape, for coin was gathered there long after. They supposed the stranger had his share, or more, and that he secreted a quantity of specie near his cabin. After his death gold was found under his clothing in a girdle.

He was often received at the houses of the fishermen, both because the people were hospitable and because they feared harm if they refused to feed or shelter him; but if his company grew wearisome he was exorcised by reading aloud a portion of the Bible. When he heard the holy words he invariably departed.

And it was said that fiends came to him at night, for in his room, whether he appeared to sleep or wake, there were groans and blasphemy, uncanny words and sounds that stirred the hair of listeners on their scalps. The unhappy creature cried to be delivered from his tormentors and begged to be spared from seeing a rehearsal of the murders he had committed.

For some time he was missed from his haunts, and it was thought that he had secured a ship and set to sea again; but a traveler on the sands, while passing his cabin in the small hours, had heard a more than usual commotion, and could distinguish the voice of the wild man raised in frantic appeal to somebody, or something; still, knowing that it was his habit to cry out so, and having misgivings about approaching the house, the traveler only hurried past.

A few neighbors went to the lonely cabin and looked through the windows which, as well as the doors, were locked on the inside. The wild man lay still and white on the floor, with the furniture upset and pieces of gold clutched in his fingers and scattered about. There were marks of claws about his neck.

The pirate ship captained by Black Sam Bellamy which Skinner refers to in his opening sentence was the famous (variously spelled) *Whidaw*—subject of a recent book: *Expedition Whydah* (highly recommended). The captive whose "false pilotage" caused its wreck—on April 16, 1717—was the captain of the whaler *Mary Anne*, who deliberately led his captured ship and the following pirate vessel onto the outer bar of Wellfleet Harbor. Most of the pirates were drowned; seven who survived were promptly hanged.

Verrill (in *Along New England Shores*) writes, "It would seem that at least one pirate escaped both the sea and the noose, for regularly every spring for years after the wreck, a villainous looking, singular stranger appeared on the Cape. Who he was no one knew, but as he spent most of his time wandering along the sands and taking bearings, everybody was convinced that he was one of Bellamy's crew, perhaps the pirate captain himself."

No Human Tie
(Boone Island, Maine)

The following is another little gem taken from Celia Thaxter's delightful little book, *Among the Isles of Shoals* (which as aforementioned was published in 1873). Is it a ghost story, I wonder? Or is suicide (by jumping off the ship) implied? Or did the deeply depressed narrator simply find a secret place on board to go off to and be by himself?

from AMONG THE ISLES OF SHOALS
by
Celia Thaxter

Boone Island is the forlornest place that can be imagined. The Isles of Shoals, barren as they are, seem like Gardens of Eden in comparison. I chanced to hear last summer of a person who had been born and brought up there; he described the loneliness as something absolutely fearful, and declared it had pursued him all through his life. He lived there till fourteen or fifteen years old, when his family moved to York.

While living on the island he discovered some human remains which had lain there thirty years. A carpenter and his assistants, having finished some building, were capsized in getting off, and all were drowned, except the master. One body floated to Plumb Island at the mouth of the Merrimack; the others the master secured, made a box for them—all the while alone—and buried them in a cleft and covered them with stones. These stones the sea washed away, and thirty years after they were buried, the boy found the bones, which were removed to York and there buried again.

It was on board a steamer bound to Bangor that the man told his story. Boone Island Light was shining in the distance. He spoke with bitterness of his life in that terrible solitude, and of "the loneliness which had pursued him ever since." All his relatives were dead, he said, and he had no human tie in the world except his wife.

He ended by anathematizing all islands, and vanishing into the darkness was not to be found again; nor did his name or any trace of him transpire, though he was sought for in the morning all about the vessel. 𝕯

THESE HAUNTED ISLES
(The Isles of Shoals, Maine and New Hampshire)

At night, sometimes, in a glory of moonlight, a vessel passed close in with all sail set, and only just air enough to fill the canvas, enough murmur from the full tide to drown the sound of her movement—a beautiful ghost stealing softly by, and passing in mysterious light beyond the glimmering headland out of sight.— Celia Thaxter

"On the Massachusetts records," Celia Thaxter tells us, "there is a paragraph to the effect that in the year 1653 Philip Babb, of Hog Island, was appointed constable for all the islands of Shoals, Star Island excepted." This, presumably, is the only historical record of our "Old Bob," "Bab," or "Babb," as he is variously named. Concerning the old reprobate, however, Thaxter has the following to relate:

119

from AMONG THE ISLES OF SHOALS
by
Celia Thaxter

There is a superstition among the islanders that Philip Babb, or some evil-minded descendent of his, still haunts Appledore; and no consideration would induce the more timid to walk alone after dark over a certain shingly beach on that island, at the top of a cove bearing Babb's name—for there the uneasy spirit is oftenest seen.

He is supposed to have been so desperately wicked when alive that there is no rest for him in his grave. His dress is a coarse, striped butcher's frock, with a leather belt, to which is attached a sheath containing a ghostly knife, sharp and glittering, which it is his delight to brandish in the face of terrified humanity.

[Thaxter next relates one or two tales of her fellow islanders' encounters with Philip Babb.] I never saw Babb, nor ever could, I think. The whole Babb family are buried in the valley of Appledore where the houses stand, and till this year a bowling alley stood upon the spot, and all the balls rolled over the bones of all the Babbs; that may have been one reason why the head of the family was so restless. Since the last equinoctial gale blew the building down, perhaps he may rest more peacefully.

[Leaving the hapless spirit of Babb to its own devices, Thaxter moves on, to a subject that calls to mind several of the ghostly pirates—Kidd, Teach, and others—already mentioned in these tales of New England hauntings.]

There is a superstition here and along the coast to this effect. A man gathering driftwood or whatever it may be, sees a spade stuck in the ground as if inviting him to dig. He isn't quite ready, goes and empties his basket first, then comes back to investigate, and lo! there's nothing there, and he is tormented the rest of his life with the thought that probably untold wealth lay beneath that spade, which he might have possessed had he only been wise enough to seize the treasure when it offered itself.

A certain man named William Mace, living at Star, long, long ago, swore that he had this experience; and there's a dim tradition that another person, seeing the spade, passed by about his business, but hastening back, arrived just in time to see the last of the sinking tool, and to perceive also a golden flat-iron disappearing into the earth. This he seized, but no human power could extricate it from the ground, and he was forced to let go his hold and see it sink out of his longing ken. 🝱

THE SHRIEKING WOMAN
(Marblehead, Massachusetts)

The recovery of many scattered legendary waifs that not only have a really important bearing upon the early history of our country, but that also shed much light upon the spirit of its ancient laws and upon the domestic lives of its people, has seemed to me a laudable undertaking . . . Samuel Adams Drake, A Book of New England Legends and Folk Lore

One of the "legendary waifs" included in Skinner's *Myths & Legends of Our Own Land* is the story of The Shrieking Woman. Skinner's book was published in 1896. Samuel Adams Drake's *A Book of New England Legends and Folk Lore*, however, appeared twelve years earlier, in 1884, and it is his version of the story that I include here.

123

"The Shrieking Woman"
by
Samuel Adams Drake

It was said that during the latter part of the seventeenth century, a Spanish ship laden with rich merchandise was captured by pirates, who brought their prize into the Harbor of Marblehead. The crew and every person on board the ill-fated ship had been butchered in cold blood at the time of the capture, except a beautiful English lady, whom the ruffians brought on shore near what is now called Oakum Bay, and there, under cover of the night, most barbarously murdered her.

The few fishermen who inhabited the place were then absent, and the women and children who remained could do nothing to prevent the consummation of the fearful crime. The piercing screams of the victim were most appalling, and her cries of "Lord, save me! Mercy! O Lord Jesus, save me!" were distinctly heard in the silence of the night. The body was buried on the spot where the deed was perpetrated, and for over one hundred and fifty years, on each anniversary of the dreadful tragedy, the heartrending screams of the murdered woman for mercy were repeated in a voice so shrill and unearthly as to freeze the blood of those who heard them.

The legend is so firmly rooted in Marblehead, that Polyphemus himself could not tear it from the soil. Even the most intelligent people have admitted their full belief in it; and one of the most learned jurists of his time, who was native here, and to the manner born, averred that he had heard those ill-omened shrieks again and again in the still hours of the night.

Once again Verrill has information to add. Referring to the Screeching Woman of Oakum Bay, he writes: "Many are those who declared they had heard the fearsome, hair-raising, unearthly sounds, and even Chief Justice Story claimed he had heard them. &

THE HOUSE ON WINNETUXET ROAD
(Plympton, Massachusetts)

. . . the queer feeling at the back of her head persisted, and now, as well as the sense of cold there was a sense of movement, as though a very cold hand were gently lifting and caressing the curls of her hair. —Norah Lofts, "Mr. Edward"

Nothing can induce Rosalie Porche to return to the house on Winnetuxet Road. Too many bad things have happened there; and in the past whenever she revisited the old Santos homestead bad luck was sure to follow.

Her family moved into the house—which was built on the site of an ancient burial ground—in 1944 when Rosalie was one year old.

She remembers the many stone markers that lay scattered throughout the blueberry patch in the woods out back. She believes that the circumstance of the house having been built on sacred Indian ground may account for at least some of the hauntings and other strange events that have occurred there throughout the years.

She cannot recall a time when the house did not feel haunted. "There was always a sense that spirits were around," she told me when I interviewed her for this story.

I should mention that I've known Rosalie for quite a long time, at least twenty years; we used to work together for the Commonwealth of Massachusetts. I've been a guest at her house in New Bedford. I've seen her daughter, Ronelle Helme, grow from a precocious child into a beautiful, accomplished young woman (at the time of this writing a student at Northeastern University). Throughout the two decades of our friendship Rosalie has been consistent in the stories she's told about the haunted house she grew up in.

"The activity would most often begin in the evening, usually after four. The steps leading into the attic would creak; curtains

would move—even when there was no breeze whatsoever. We'd hear chunks of wood being tossed into the stove—when of course there was nobody there. Sometimes at night as we lay in bed invisible hands would tug at the coverings. Worst of all we'd see shadows—spirits—moving from room to room. They'd float like sheets. Or like fog passing."

Her daughter, Ronelle, has seen the floating shapes, too—on numerous occasions. She describes what she saw as "shadows. Forms without faces."

Although as a young child and even as a teenager Rosalie was terrified of the shadows and would not stay alone in the house, her mother, Rose Santos, didn't seem troubled by them.

"They're just my people," she would say. When they became a nuisance she would simply order them to "go away."

There was one occasion, however, when Mrs. Santos had to take more drastic action. This was in 1946 when Rosalie was three years old. She, her mother, and her Aunt Mary were alone in the house. Suddenly something—the devil? or perhaps a demon?—appeared outside at the window peering in. "It was hairy, like a bear, with horns and it had big bold red eyes." All three of them saw it.

"May God take you straight to hell!" her mother shouted in Crioulo (the language of Cape Verde), upon which the demon raced around the house three times then disappeared. Whatever it was—devil, demon, or mirage—they never saw it again.

The same cannot be said about the ghostly palomino which Rosalie and two of her sisters (Joanne and Bertha)—and later, Ronelle—saw time and time again. Rosalie was thirteen the first time she saw the equine apparition, which she describes as "*solid*—not *shadowy* like the other spirits." The horse would suddenly appear galloping down the hallway from the kitchen.

Ronelle first saw it when she was six. "It galloped from the kitchen just as I was putting the light on in the living room." She felt an intense cold, followed by a gust of wind, then it was gone.

Some spots in the house were worse than others, Rosalie recalls. The bathroom was one of the bad locations, where "you would always feel as if you were being watched." Worst of all was the attic. Rosalie would never venture there alone.

She recalls an inexplicable event related to the attic that occurred when she was quite young. While she and her sister Bertha and one or two of her other siblings (all told, there were eight children in the Santos family) were playing they found an ancient chest hidden in a crawl space in a remote corner. Inside the chest they found "some Indian beads" and an ancient tome, a dusty brown book dating, she believes, from the early eighteen hundreds. The children carried the book and the beads downstairs and left them over night in the kitchen. The next morning they were gone. They simply vanished, never to be seen again.

The day after Rosalie's father died, her sister-in-law saw him sitting at the kitchen table.

Her brother Roger was once sitting outside in his truck and saw "something" in an upstairs window. Suddenly, from nowhere, a hubcap struck his truck.

Several years ago a real estate agent looking through the house abruptly ran from it in terror. To this day he refuses to talk about what he saw that so frightened him.

The above are only a few of the many weird things that have taken place in the house on Winnetuxet Road. When I asked Rosalie what was the worst thing that ever happened to her there, she did not hesitate but immediately related an incident that occurred when she was about forty years old.

She was going out the door to do some shopping for her

mother. Her sister Joanne was with her. All of a sudden she felt a spirit go through her body; she became ill and couldn't walk.

"My mother found it amusing. She began to laugh. I had my sister take me to the hospital. But the doctors said there was nothing at all wrong with me."

Strange things like that were always happening. Often, cars parked in the yard wouldn't start. Mechanics would examine them and find nothing amiss. As soon as the vehicles were towed away from the property they would run without a hitch

When Ronelle was fifteen she had a pet dog that adored her. It was a beagle with one blue eye and one green eye. Ronelle and the dog were inseparable. One day, when she was visiting her grandmother on Winnetuxet Road, the dog suddenly went berserk and without provocation turned on her. Its eyes—the blue eye and the green eye—glowed red, as if it were possessed. Later the dog disappeared from the property, perhaps stolen . . .

Rosalie recites a whole litany of misfortunes that have happened to her, to her siblings, her children and other family members, and to friends and strangers alike at the house on Winnetuxet Road. Most notable was the mishap involving her sister, Irma. When little Irma was five years old she wandered off and became lost in the woods. She wasn't found until two days later. It was winter, the nights were cold, and the child was badly frost-bitten. Fortunately the story has a happy ending (you can read about it in Lena Britto's memoirs, *Yankee Mericana*) but it does typify the bad luck that Rosalie feels is associated with the house.

On the other hand, people have lived there for years on end without anything bad happening. It's possible that the so-called "bad luck" is only typical of the vicissitudes that normally occur within a large family. It's also possible that the house is no longer haunted.

At least one of the ghosts, it seems, has left the house.

131

It followed Rosalie all the way to New Bedford.

Sometime after her mother died, Rosalie was at home in New Bedford talking on the phone to her sister Joanne. Without warning, she saw her mother stomp out of her (Rosalie's) bedroom and move down the hallway.

After that Rosalie's luck seemed to change for the better. She came into some money unexpectedly and was able to pay off some nagging bills, and other good things began to happen. Evidently the spirit of her mother—who always got along with the spirits in the house on Winnetuxet Road—is looking after her.

"She Must Go Back."
(Cohasset, Massachusetts)

Although Trish lived in a haunted house for a while (many years ago, in Wollaston, Massachusetts) and presently owns a centuries-old building that boasts a number of restless spirits, hers is not, strictly speaking, a ghost story.

And Trish—an active, healthy, successful mother, wife, and businesswoman—is certainly not herself a ghost. She's very much alive: despite the fact that when she was nineteen years old she apparently crossed—for several crucial minutes—the boundary between life and death.

It was late at night. She had just left work. When she arrived home, an acquaintance offered her a ride on the back of his motorcycle. She accepted—much to her regret. He was a foolish young man and immediately began to show off, driving recklessly at a high speed. Despite her pleas he refused to slow down or drive more cautiously, and the inevitable happened. On the way

133

from Hull to Cohasset, on Jerusalem Road, he lost control and they crashed into a stone wall.

It was a horrific crash. They bounced off the wall several times (and in the process destroyed at least ten rose bushes). Trish remembers being flung from the motorcycle—"I was flipped like a card"—and landing on her back. Later, she learned that she not only suffered a total of twenty-six fractures but also lost the skin from her back "down to my bones."

As she lay on the pavement all was quiet. She felt no pain. Then she began to hear people whispering. She could see, but only as if through a fog. She found herself in the center of a circle of ornate seats on which were seated distinguished-looking men and women. All the while she felt the sensation of having no body.

The men and women in the seats surrounding her were discussing bits and pieces of her life. In Trish's words, "They were weighing the scales." One person or another would lean to the left or right and speak. They would mention incidents from her past. "Remember when she did . . ." one would say. "But she learned from that," someone else would answer.

Finally a man spoke: "It's time. We must decide a fate."

"She must go back," a woman said. "To parent the child of a sibling."

"So be it!"

When Trish awoke, an EMT was pushing on her chest, trying to revive her. She heard the words " . . .no vital signs."

It took her six months to recover from the accident. She was told that she would never walk again. For a month and a half she wore a metal halo—and a neck collar long after that. Despite what the doctors said, Trish was determined to fully recover, and after months of physical therapy she did.

134

In the meantime she talked about her otherworldly experience: the circle of men and women who—as she lay in a bodiless sate— debated her fate. The doctors assumed that she was psychologically disturbed and sent her for psychiatric evaluation. She passed with flying colors, of course.

And was eventually vindicated.

Seven years after the accident—and the pronouncement that "She must go back, to parent the child of a sibling."—she became, through a series of circumstances, the adoptive parent of her niece, her sister's daughter.

Today Trish owns and operates a thriving business—The Absent Innkeeper—in the quiet seaside village of Manomet, in Plymouth, Massachusetts. The building that houses her office and gift shop dates back at least to the seventeen hundreds; part of it once served as a school, part as a chapel, and there is evidence that it was an important stop on the Underground Railroad, providing temporary sanctuary to dozens of fugitive slaves.

The building is haunted. But that is a story for another time. (Trish is still researching its history.)

"What happened to the young man on the motorcycle whose reckless behavior caused you so much suffering?" I asked Trish when I interviewed her for this book.

"He sprained his ankle," she answered, dryly. "And never apologized for what he did." ⊕

Moonlight Harvest
(Wareham, Massachusetts)

As I have mentioned elsewhere (in Deep Meadow Bog *and in its sequel,* Cranberry Chronicles*), Mr. Barnes lived deep in the woods in a decaying house near an abandoned cranberry bog, without benefit of electricity or running water and with Ticklebelly—an aging, rheumatic cat—his sole companion. In the early 1950's—when I was eight, nine, ten, eleven, twelve—it was still a neighborhood tradition, the last day of October, for us kids to ride our bicycles across town to enjoy our elderly friend's hospitality and to listen to his "scary but true" ghost stories.*

Just how true—or if you prefer, just how factual "Moonlight Harvest" is, I cannot honestly say. At one time I believed that the events as related by Mr. Barnes occurred exactly as he described them. After all, would Mr. Barnes—a hero in the trenches of World War I, a man who had survived the Great Depression, a man who drank only the finest rotgut whiskey—would such a man lie?

I could, I suppose, research old newspapers for accounts that would corroborate the historicity of some of the incidents

137

mentioned by Mr. Barnes in his story. But that would take a great deal of time—I'm not sure of the exact year, nor for that matter the exact decade, of the occurrences. And what if I found no mention of any of the events that he mentioned? What would that prove, other than that either my memory, or my research methods, were faulty?

As a memento of his younger days Mr. Barnes kept on his doorstep the carapace of a huge snapping turtle.

He'd captured the turtle one day during the Great Depression while working on the cranberry bogs. After work he transported it home in the back of his pickup and plopped it into an old barrel, where he fattened it up with garbage before killing and eating it. He used the carapace—which in the eyes of us kids merited comparison with an army tank from World War II—as a doorstop. Every time we crossed the threshold we glanced down at the gruesome relic and shuddered, recalling that this was the very turtle that had caused Mr. Barnes to, in his own words, "turn cannibal."

Grasping the huge snapper by its tail, Mr. Barnes had grown careless and allowed it to take a chunk out of his arm with its powerful jaws. (He still bore the scar and would roll up his sleeve every once in awhile to remind us—and himself, he said—of his folly.) By a process of ratiocination eminently logical to the juvenile intellect, Mr. Barnes concluded that eating the meat of a turtle that had once taken a bite out of him made *him*—Mr. Barnes—a cannibal.

Though imbued with more than his share of holiday spirit, Mr. Barnes did not decorate his property for Halloween. He saw no need for such superfluous habiliments as pumpkins carved into jack-o'-lanterns or bed sheets sewn into the shapes of ghosts. His house—situated at the end of a lonely dirt road, encased in shadows, surrounded by swampland and dense brush, with only a soot-encrusted oil lamp and the glow from a smoldering wood fire to dispel the gloom—seemed spooky enough.

To lend atmosphere to his ghost stories, Mr. Barnes had at his disposal any number of natural sound effects: the hooing of an owl, the barking of a fox, the cries of nocturnal creatures being pounced upon and devoured by predators. Add dead leaves skittering across the forest floor; the wind soughing through coniferous boughs; and branches swaying aloft, creaking against one another; and you had all the accouterments essential to a scary evening.

As we huddled around the kitchen table it was not merely what we heard, but also (and more especially) what we *didn't* hear, that contributed to the creepiness. Lacking electricity and running water—and the appliances dependent upon them—Mr. Barnes's house lacked those everyday sounds that might otherwise have given us a sense of cozy domesticity.

Unlike a refrigerator, an icebox doesn't hum, or vibrate, or jostle bottles and jars with frequent and cheerful *clinks*. Nor does a wood stove kick on, clatter and clank as if about to fall apart, then abruptly shut down—constantly calling attention to itself— the way an aging oil burner does.

Despite the crackle of flames and the occasional hiss of escaping gas, a wood stove—like an icebox—conspires to an atmosphere of absolute, and eerie, silence.

A silence conducive to the telling of ghost stories.

As I grew older I never entirely stopped visiting Mr. Barnes, even when visiting him had become no longer fashionable. He was, after all, a friend.

But as the years passed by (years increasingly devoted to pursuing an education, along with the funds needed to pay for it) my visits became less frequent. Whenever I did drop by it was mainly to say hello and to ascertain that all was well. Too often I would cut my visit short with the excuse (genuine but not pardonable) that I was on my way to somewhere else.

One season of Halloween, though—when I was in my late teens or early twenties (memory is vague regarding exactly when; but it is safe to say it was some forty years ago)—I made up my mind to pay a proper visit.

It was late evening, and although the date was not precisely October 31 the moon was waxing toward the full. Canada geese flocking south in jagged vees honked high overhead; smoke from burning leaves scented the air; and smashed pumpkins littered the asphalt streets, orange on black, emblem of All Hallow's Eve.

That evening, seated at the kitchen table with a plateful of oatmeal cookies conveniently placed between us (they had been baked fresh that afternoon by Mr. Barnes in his Dutch oven), we chatted for a while and caught up on various topics, such as my progress at school and Mr. Barnes's progress at the art of living alone in the woods. Then, in the flickering glow of the oil lamp, with Ticklebelly curled in the corner by the wood stove, Mr. Barnes—having first lubricated his throat with a shot of rotgut whiskey—leaned back in his chair and unfolded a ghost story.

Just like in the old days.

The only difference between this time and then was, instead of an audience of many he had an audience of one.

140

By way of preamble he cleared his (by now liberally lubricated) throat.

"Most likely you've heard the expression 'moonlight harvesters?'"

I nodded. "People who steal cranberries by scooping someone else's bog at night. The moon gives 'em just enough light to see by."

"A moon just like tonight's," Mr. Barnes said. "Full, or darn close to it."

At the end of a dead-end dirt road, with no neighbors other than the wild creatures that lived—and died—in the surrounding swamp, Mr. Barnes had no need for curtains or window shades. Moonbeams splashed freely through the upper portions of the east-facing window—and illustrated, as it were, the context of his speech.

"When I was young—maybe about your age—I worked for a cranberry grower named . . . well, let's just call him 'Old Skinflint.' If I mentioned his real name you might recognize it, even though he's been dead for quite a long time. As a Latin scholar you're no doubt familiar with the expression *De mortuis nil nisi bonu*: 'Of the dead, speak nothing but good.' I'd be hard pressed to say anything good about Old Skinflint. But if I refrained from saying anything bad, why there'd be no story. So I'll compromise, and let the fellow remain anonymous.

"Old Skinflint—or 'Skinflint' for short—owned a bunch of cranberry bogs, some down the Cape, a couple here in Wareham, and one or two in Middleborough. After he died they were parceled out to his nieces and nephews, most of whom I'm happy to say are decent human beings—something Old Skinflint certainly wasn't. He earned his sobriquet by being the meanest tightwad in the county.

"Skinflint was I'd say in his mid fifties when he took me on as his right-hand man. He looked a lot older, though, with thinning

141

white hair and a sallow complexion. And he looked gaunt—as if he didn't eat right. Tall, in excess of six feet, but giving the appearance of being much shorter. That's because he walked all stooped over, with his head bent low—as if by not looking people straight in the eye all his life he'd ruined his posture. Or maybe I'm reading too much into it. Maybe he walked that way—with his eyes cast down—in hopes of spotting loose change on the ground."

"If he was such a cheapskate," I asked, "how come you agreed to work for him? Weren't you afraid he'd cheat you?"

Mr. Barnes chuckled. "He paid me a salary, which I made damn sure I collected every Saturday.

"Hell, the most he could've gypped me out of was one week's pay—which you can rest assured, if he ever tried anything fancy, I'd have gotten out of him one way or the other. But the reason he never tried to hoodwink *me* was simple: he'd cheated so many folks over the years, nobody else in town would work for him. Without me, who'd help him out on frost nights? Who'd stay up until two a.m. gallivanting around from one bog to another checking thermometers and starting irrigation pumps?"

"And you didn't mind being in his employ?"

Mr. Barnes grunted. "'Being in his employ.' Is that a fancy way of saying, 'working for him?'"

"Well, yeah."

Mr. Barnes reached for the whiskey bottle. "Don't mind me," he apologized, and took a swig. "I'm picking on you to cover up my own feelings of guilt. Truth is, the only reason I worked for Old Skinflint was so I could be foreman—and have my own crew of greenhorns to boss around. Every year he took on a fresh batch, mostly Portuguese from the Cape Verde Islands. They'd stay for a season or two. Then, soon as they figured out they could do a hell of a lot better elsewhere, they'd move on.

"To tempt men to stay till the end of the season some of the

142

bigger growers provided housing. Not to be outdone, Skinflint got hold of a couple of old tumble-down shacks which he moved to a clearing and joined together to form what he called a house, though it was scarcely more than a set of flimsy walls with a roof and partitions. He tossed in a half dozen second-hand bunks (some of which he'd rescued from the town dump) and drove a pipe into the ground with a hand pump for water.

"The first summer I worked for Skinflint he had me spruce up the shack for that fall's occupants. 'They'll need a new stove,' I pointed out, after I'd nailed down a half dozen loose floorboards and patched a couple of holes in the roof. 'This old potbelly has about had it.'

"Skinflint looked at me as if I'd suggested installing a marble fireplace or even a central heating system. ''Taint nothing wrong with that stove.'

"'There's plenty wrong with it,' I said. 'The metal's rusted and worn so thin you could poke your fist through. It ain't safe. It's a fire hazard. It may be okay to heat water with, if they keep a constant eye on it. But for warmth on a cold night — unwatched—it could burn the place down.'

"'It's good enough for a bunch of Portagees,' was Skinflint's reply. 'If they don't like the stove I provide for 'em they can damn well bring their own.'

"'Then the least you can do is let me lay some bricks in this area, just in case the stove does overheat,' I said. 'That way—'

"Before I could say another word Skinflint let loose with some choice epithets, telling me in no uncertain terms where I could shove my bricks.

"'Mind your own business,' he finally told me, when I tried once more to reason with him.

"I got so mad I almost quit then and there. God knows I wish I had. But like I say, I was young and foolish, and swell-headed with being foreman. Even so, to spite Old Skinflint I spent the

143

better part of the following day painting the interior of the "house," so it would look a little bit more welcoming to the men, a couple of whom were scarcely more than boys, who would be living for the first time in a foreign land, so far away from families and friends.

"By the end of August Skinflint had persuaded five young men—fresh from the island of Brava with hardly a dozen words of English between them—to stay and work through the harvest season. He lured them by providing living quarters free of charge and by promising high wages—wages which, judging from prior experience, he would in the end avoid paying by claiming that, because of their imperfect knowledge of the language, the men had misunderstood the amount agreed upon."

Mr. Barnes paused, and cast a mournful eye at the nearly empty pint bottle which lay propped against a stack of dirty dishes next to the dry-sink. (To do him justice, I should mention that at the start of my visit the bottle had been only slightly more than a third full.)

As if to wipe away the taste of temptation he drew his sleeve across his mouth. With an effort he refrained from what was no doubt uppermost in his mind—the desire to seize the bottle and polish it off in one fell swoop.

"By the end of September I got to know those fellers pretty well. Big Manny and Little Manny, Joe, Jake, and Peter. Hard workers, all of them. From what I understood of their language, I gathered that they were saving up most of their money to send back to their folks in Cape Verde.

"As to their 'home' here in the good old US of A—the shanty on the edge of the bog—I should've warned them about that

144

defective stove. But if the truth be told I'd forgot all about it. The last two weeks of September we saw a spell of warm weather. Wood stoves was the subject furthest from my mind. Besides, I was busy harvesting cranberries. Not to mention manning the pumps for frost when the night temperatures returned to normal.

"That's my excuse, anyhow. For not doing something about that stove."

Mr. Barnes reached over, seized the pint bottle, and tossing back his head drained it dry.

"Around the last day of September the warm spell ended. On a couple of nights I had to start the irrigation pumps to prevent frost damage. Hailing from off the coast of Africa, those fellers weren't used to freezing temperatures. They kept that wood stove fired up at all times. One night—the second week in October—the shack caught fire and burned to the ground.

"When I swung by in the morning to cart the men off to work the shack was gone—reduced to just a heap of smoldering ashes. From the back of the pickup I grabbed a potato digger (which I used for clearing trash racks on the pump houses) and poked around. I found enough to show me what my nose had already hinted at: that the men hadn't escaped.

"I drove to the nearest phone and notified the police. Then I drove back to the site and waited. Once the police and fire truck arrived, I didn't hang around to watch; I drove to the bog we were harvesting that day and told Skinflint about the fire.

"He was upset. Not so much by the death of five men, but because now he had to go out and find replacements for them.

"I was still pretty much shaken up. All I could think of was those five fellers: their charred remains. Big Manny and Little Manny. Joe, Jake, and Peter. And I thought about their families back in Cape Verde.

"'The police will notify their families through the Consulate, I guess,' I said to Skinflint. 'You can probably send their pay

145

through the Consulate, too.'

"'What pay?'

"'The money you owe them.'

"Skinflint scowled. 'I don't owe nobody nothing. If anything, *they* owe me. For burning down my building. Careless smoking, most likely.'

"'Careless smoking my eye! It was that stove, and you know it.'

"Well, Old Skinflint just turned and walked away, muttering. That was his way of dismissing the whole matter. I made up my mind then and there that that was the last I'd work for the old buzzard. I'd finish out the season—it would go against my grain to see perfectly good berries rot on the vines, which I knew would most likely happen if I didn't stay. But once the berries were picked, that would be it. And I'd make damn sure anyone who did go to work for him would know just what they were getting themselves into.

"The setback caused by the deaths of those five fellers extended the harvest season into November. The bog where they died was the last to be picked.

"On the morning of October 31st I arrived shortly after dawn. As soon as I rounded the bend by the clearing where the shack had been I knew something was amiss. The pyramid of empties I'd stacked on shore the day before was gone. I jumped the shore ditch and examined the vines, which had that rumpled look they get, after harvesting, from being tugged at.

"I found vines, but no berries.

"Sometime during the night a crew of 'moonlight harvesters' had hand-scooped an entire acre. Funny thing, though—I didn't see any tire tracks from the truck that must have carted the berries away.

"Well, you can imagine Skinflint's reaction when I told him an acre's worth of his crop had been stolen. He was hopping mad.

"'Must have been a half dozen of 'em,' he mused, after he'd reported the theft to the police and calmed down a bit. 'It'd take at least that many scoopers to pick that many berries in so short a time.'

"'They had plenty of light to see by,' I said. 'Almost a full moon. And no clouds. Looks like the same for tonight.'

"'We'd best stand guard,' Skinflint said. 'With shotguns.'

"Skinflint lived in one of those stately old mansions on High Street built by ship's captains; he'd inherited it from his parents. He lived alone. (I'd heard a rumor that he'd been married once, but treated his wife so mean she'd left him after only a couple of months. But maybe that was just malicious gossip.)

"I swung by to pick him up after supper.

"I'd forgot it was Halloween until I saw all the kids in their costumes trick-or-treating up and down the streets. Skinflint, of course, wasn't about to waste money on candy for kids, so he'd kept all his lights off and was sitting in the dark when I arrived. I had to feel my way down the walkway and almost broke my neck when I tripped over a garden urn.

"When I rang the doorbell curtains parted and a pasty face with squinting eyes appeared in the window.

"'Dammit, it's me,' I shouted.

"He opened the door and without a word of greeting thrust a shotgun into my hands. 'It's loaded,' he said. He reached to one side and grabbed another that was leaning against the wainscot. 'So's this one.' Joining me in the darkness, he locked the door behind him.

"I let him walk in front of me. If one of us was going to stumble and accidentally shoot the other in the back, I'd rather it was me than him."

Mr. Barnes stood up from his chair, stretched his legs, and walked over to the window where the moon shining through splashed its beams—as if from a bottomless bucket—onto the kitchen floor. He stood there for a long while, basking in the liquid light, and gazed at the sky.

"Moon just like tonight," he said, more to himself than to me.

Then, gathering his thoughts: "When we got to the bog, after driving through the woods down the long dirt road that led to it, there was a full moon hanging in the sky, just like now. It looked like a huge electric light somebody had strung there, deliberately, to illuminate the bog.

"'Plenty of moonlight to see by,' Skinflint said. 'Besides, they probably obtained extra visibility by shining the headlights from their vehicles onto the vines.'

"'Strange,' I said. 'I didn't notice any tire tracks.'

"'Well it ain't likely they carried off the boxes on their backs,' Skinflint remarked.

"'Speaking of what ain't likely,' I said, 'do you really think they'll return tonight? They must figure we'll be waiting for 'em.'

"'They might not know we're on to 'em. Or they might figure we'd figure they wouldn't come back.' He shrugged. 'I ain't taking no chances.'

"We left the pickup hidden behind a clump of maples by the pump house next to the river and walked back to the bog, where we sat on a fallen log in the shadows at the edge of the clearing where the shanty had stood. Skinflint held his shotgun cradled in his arms. I leaned mine next to me against the log but kept my fingers against the stock. We had a clear view of the bog as far as the first dike.

"It had rained since the fire; a fetor of damp charcoal tainted the air. Damp charcoal and something else. Something intangible, but close enough to the stench of death to turn my stomach and make me sick."

Mr. Barnes left the window and, grudgingly it seemed, returned to his chair.

"It was 'autumn in New England', of course, and the leaves had turned. In the moonlight the vivid colors faded and took on a sickly look, like artificial flowers left outside and washed pale by wind and rain.

"'This isn't going to work,' I said to Skinflint after we'd sat there for half an hour. 'It's too damn cold to sit here half the night, waiting for what most likely won't happen.'"

Mr. Barnes picked up an oatmeal cookie and idly crumbled it between his fingers as he glanced at me across the table. "You can see that my heart wasn't in it. Not that staying up all night bothered me any. It didn't. Hell, I was used to it, what with all the frost nights I'd already put in that season." Mr. Barnes shook his head. "What bothered me was the two of us. Me, sitting on a dead log in deep shadow, a mile or more from the nearest habitation, next to *him*—a man I despised. And each of us holding a loaded shotgun.

"After I'd spoken Skinflint gave me a look of disgust but kept quiet. Neither one of us had thought to bring along a Thermos of hot coffee. Even if we had I don't think I'd have drunk any. I could feel a hard knot in the pit of my stomach. If I'd swallowed coffee—or anything—I think I would've puked.

"The air temperature must have been somewhere in the mid thirties, but the wind made it feel even colder. I decided I'd give it another half hour then leave. If Skinflint wanted to stay, that would be his decision. I had the keys to the pickup and I meant to hold on to them.

"Now, I swear that neither one of us fell asleep. In the first

149

place, it was too damn cold. Every once in a while I'd have to get up and stamp my feet to keep from getting numb. And Skinflint was no different; if anything he fidgeted worse than me. And we were sitting on a rotting log; if we'd nodded off, we'd have keeled over backwards or lurched to one side and immediately wakened up. So don't ask me how a solid two hours could've passed without me realizing it. Or how the two of us could've missed seeing—*them*.

"The first thing I noticed was the moon. It had shifted position. That is to say it had climbed higher in the sky, and lit up a wide swathe directly in front of us. From where we sat we had a clear view of the bog, almost as if we were in a movie theater looking at an image on the screen.

"And then—as if a lens had been adjusted so that the image came into focus—I spotted the thieves: on the bog, on their knees hard at work, gliding the tines of their wooden scoops through the vines with a rocking motion. At first they appeared to be mere shadows. But as I stared they gradually took on a pale luminescence—as if they were being sketched in and painted by an invisible artist.

"Skinflint saw them about the same time I did. Shotgun in hand he bolted from the log and lunged forward. Without taking my eyes off the thieves I groped around for my gun, which I'd somehow let fall onto the ground. I located it by the coldness of the barrel, and grabbing it stood upright.

"But then I froze.

"It wasn't stiffness from having sat on the log for so long; it was fear—pure and unadulterated—that prevented me from moving even an inch. Anyone who hasn't seen—what I saw—can scoff. But till it happens to you, take my word. I was scared nearly witless. And *physically* unable to move.

"I give myself credit, though, for managing to open my mouth to shout a warning to Skinflint. The damn fool was plunging

150

headlong across the clearing toward the bog and the thieves. Silhouetted against the sky, he looked like a scarecrow that had suddenly come to life, or a crazed combatant charging across some forgotten No Man's Land.

"'There's five of 'em,' I yelled. 'Don't you recognize who they are? Big Manny and Little Manny and Joe and Jake and Peter! It's *them*.'

"But he didn't hear me. Or wasn't listening. Or didn't give a hoot.

"'I'll fix 'em!' he shouted and began blasting away with both barrels.

"Unfazed, the five men—I won't call them thieves; they were after all only taking what was owed to them—the five men went on with their work, as if Skinflint was just an amused spectator, or a casual passerby, and not a madman intent on blasting them away with a shotgun.

"And he was a madman, I swear. I think at some point there came upon him the realization of what they were, and of what *he* was, and what he had done and not done. And it caused him to snap.

"As he raced across the clearing toward the bog he kept stopping to reload and fire, even though the blasts were having no effect whatsoever. But when he came to the ditch he didn't even pause but kept on running and stumbled headlong into it. And—it appears, from the autopsy the coroner later performed on his body—broke his neck.

"Fell and broke his neck. That's what the coroner's report said. But that's not how I saw it.

"How I saw it was, he cleared the ditch and ran right up to Big Manny, and it was Big Manny who left off scooping berries long enough to seize hold of Skinflint by the throat and twist his neck around until it snapped. Then he flung the body into the ditch, like it was a piece of trash, and resumed scooping.

151

"In those days, you see," Mr. Barnes said a bit later, after he'd poured himself a swig from a freshly opened bottle, "even as now, there were unscrupulous growers who were willing to accept stolen cranberries and sell them as their own and spilt the profits with the thieves. Don't ask me how they managed it, but I'm convinced that those five fellers—the *ghosts* of those five fellers—harvested the berries from that bog in order to get the money Skinflint owned them (as well as the money that, by dying, they would not be earning in years to come) in order to send it back home to their folks in Cape Verde.

"I hightailed it out of there, of course, and concocted a story to explain to the police what had happened. At first they thought I was pulling a Halloween prank, or that I was drunk—I guess I wasn't acting all that rational, after what I'd seen—but I finally convinced them that they'd better go and check up on Old Skinflint. And like I said, they found him in the ditch, with his neck broken.

"Funny thing, though—the next morning another acre of crop was missing.

"And I'll tell you something else. Scared as I was, the next night I went back, and waited—this time in the pickup with the motor running and the heater on—and sure enough they showed up again. Only this time there were six of them.

"Big Manny and Little Manny, and Joe and Jake and Peter. And Skinflint, on his knees, scooping away along side of them.

"And I'll tell you another thing. Skinflint looked different from the others. The other five shone sort of pale, like congealed moonlight. But Skinflint seemed to glow, sort of red and yellow, as if with a flickering flame. As if he was fighting an internal fire and could keep himself from burning up only by pitching in and scooping like a madman.

"I didn't go back after that. But I heard, as the years passed, that those acres never would produce again. The nephew who inherited that particular bog finally gave up and sold it for house lots." 🪦

Afterword

After all, aren't the best ghost stories the ones that enable us to suspend belief and totally immerse ourselves in the dark worlds of the storytellers? — Bernhardt J. Hurwood, Passport to the Supernatural

155

THE GHOST WARS
(FACT VERSUS FICTION)

It is luckier for a ghost to be vividly imagined than dully "experienced;" and nobody knows better than a ghost how hard it is to put him or her into words shadowy yet transparent enough.
—Edith Wharton, The Ghost Stories of Edith Wharton

"Are these stories true?"

How many hundreds—how many thousands—of times have I been asked that annoying question?

Annoying because of the implication: "If these stories are *not* true, then why are you wasting your time writing them?"

Or something to that effect.

No one ever asks Stephen King—one of the most popular and best-selling authors of all time—whether *his* stories are true. Perhaps that's because he had the good sense, from the very outset, to label his fiction "horror" rather than "ghost stories."

Factual ghost stories have their devoted following, as do made-up ghost stories. And never the twain shall meet. Or so it

157

sometimes seems. Actually I write both: stories that are absolutely true, and stories that are nothing more than figments of my (some might say over-active) imagination.

I enjoy writing—and reading—both genre.

But if I had my druthers—if I had to chose only one—it would be fictional over factual, for reading and for writing. A well-crafted ghost story—whether by a recognized master such as M.R. James, E.F. Benson, or Edith Wharton, or by my humble self— has the power to evoke all those familiar, archetypal clichés that readers or listeners so perversely love: chills running up and down our spine, shivers of apprehension wracking our frame. What caused that creaking on the stairway? that rasping against the window pane? Is there something lurking behind that curtain? And why is the dog cringing by the door?

A loaf of bread, a jug of wine, and a ghastly tale read by the flickering flames of a smoldering fire. What greater contentment can life—or for that matter, the after-life— offer?

Why then—if I'm so fond of fabricated tales—do I bother to write *true* ghost stories?

Before I attempt to answer that question let me explain why I—and millions like me—find ghost stories (of any stripe) so appealing.

Fondness for ghost stories can be attributed to the universal appeal of being scared. Life, as we know, presents many terrors that are all too real: dangers or tragedies which can instill in us feelings of helplessness. Ghost stories offer us an opportunity to be scared while at the same time feeling snugly safe.

For many of us, no doubt, this fondness has something to do with early exposure. I recall my own childhood: those autumn evenings when, huddled together in the shadows of a darkened room in an isolated house deep in the woods, my buddies and I listened to creepy tales we knew were not true—or were they? We fervently hoped they were not. After all, home for some of us was a long, lonely bicycle ride away.

Being scared yet ultimately emerging unscathed offers assurances that life is manageable, that we *can* cope with and conquer our fears.

Fine. But why prefer fictional over factual?

Well, for one thing, many true ghost stories are not really *stories*. They lack a plot: a beginning, a middle, and an end. They may also lack suspense. For example: someone glances up from reading a newspaper and sees Uncle Archie—who died five years ago—sitting in his favorite rocking chair. Then Uncle Archie abruptly vanishes.

That's it. That's the complete "story." It may be a frightening experience for the person who sees the ghost. Or of interest to those who personally knew Uncle Archie. But for us, as readers, the incident's appeal is merely in its mystery. Geewhilikens! Did someone really see a ghost? Can such things be? Or did the person just imagine the whole thing? We shrug our shoulders then turn our minds to other things.

But a fictional ghost story—skillfully narrated—may cause us to sit on the edge of our seat as our hair bristles and goose pimples sprout all over our body. Can anyone who has read "Oh, Whistle, And I'll Come to You, My Lad" ever forget the experience? M.R. James's classic ghost story not only is scary— it scared the wits out of me the first time I read it—but it also serves as a cautionary tale. Don't mess around with certain things, for you may live to regret it.

Writers of fiction enjoy freedoms which are not always available to writers of nonfiction. Fiction writers are free to manipulate, to delve into the minds of characters, to give their imaginations free rein.

In "Hideous Green"(in my collection, *Shapes That Haunt New England*) I employ the literary equivalent of slight of hand; there *is* a ghost, but not necessarily the one the reader expects.

159

Hopefully, along with a twinge of fear, I've provided an element of pleasurable surprise. In "Flume Child" (in the same volume), which some readers tell me is very scary, I present the story from the point of view of the ghost—who insists that she's not really a ghost at all. But we know better. As for giving my imagination free rein: I've actually managed to scare myself a few times.

Speaking of being scared . . .

The most chilling ghost story I've ever read—and I've read many thousands, both fictional and true—is "The Demon Lover" by Elizabeth Bowen. That the story is so memorable has a lot to do with the fact that Elizabeth Bowen was one of the great fiction writers of the twentieth century. She had complete command of the language. And knew how to spin a yarn. Unfortunately, she wrote only a handful of ghost stories.

My own preference for fiction over fact is evidenced by a true story which I presented as fiction and included in my first book of ghost stories, *Shapes That Haunt New England.* The events which I narrated in "The Ceramic Cat" really did take place. In Plymouth, Massachusetts. In the 1970's. I changed one or two minor details, primarily to tighten the plot, but otherwise I related events exactly as they happened.

What did I gain by my deception?

Well, the mood I wanted to evoke was not one of fear, but rather of loss, of sadness, of regret for what might have been. And since I was personally involved—and much shier then than I am now—I didn't want readers to know that I was the one who was feeling sad and regretful. So I made believe that the story—which was true—was only make-believe.

So—having said all this, about how and why I prefer fictional ghost stories to true ghost stories—the question remains. Why do I bother to write true ghost stories?

Well, not because true ghost stories are scary. They sometimes are. But more often they're not.

In *Haunters of the Dusk*, my first book of true ghost stories, I stressed to my readers that the more certain I was that a story was true, the more likely I was to present it in journalistic fashion. But the more skeptical I was, the more likely I was to use the techniques of fiction.

I personally know, and am friends with, the family who live in "The House of the Five Suicides." I do not doubt any of the strange and inexplicable events which, they tell me, have occurred there. And so, in recounting them, I stuck strictly to the methods a journalist would use in reporting any true story.

"The House of the Five Suicides" is without a doubt the most fascinating of all the stories included in *Haunters of the Dusk*. More than that, it provides a solution to a mystery—concerning a notorious criminal—that is more than three decades old.

But, for the most part, "The House of the Five Suicides" is not scary.

Bizarre, yes. Mind-boggling. Mysterious. Wondrous. Extraordinary. And of course—keeping in mind the suicides—tragic.

But—except for one midnight visitation—not in the least bit scary.

What then, if not its ability to frighten us, is the lure of the *true*—the *non*fiction—ghost story?

Besides satisfying a craving for the odd, the outré, the mysterious—just *who* (or perhaps one should ask, just *what*) did occupy Uncle Archie's favorite rocking chair?—the true ghost story offers a hope of sorts, at the least a suggestion, that there may be something to our human lives beyond the merely physical. We may, indeed, have a spiritual nature. There may be an existence after death. Or, if you're already a believer in the afterlife, the true ghost story is just further proof of something you've always known: That human existence transcends the mundane. That there is more to life than just getting or spending. And that the smart-ass scientists don't necessarily have all the answers. 𝕒

Appendices

Appendix One

COMMONLY ASKED QUESTIONS

A student at a middle school in Maine who was doing a research project on ghosts sent me a list of questions, which I answered to the best of my abilities. Because the questions are representative of those I'm frequently asked, at the risk of being somewhat repetitious I've included them below, along with the answers.

1. **How did you get interested in the paranormal?** Ghost stories and folklore have always fascinated me. However, it was fictional rather than factual ghost stories that caught my early interest: the stories of M.R. James, Edith Wharton, E.F. Benson, and many others. When I became a writer I naturally wrote the sort of stories I enjoyed reading, including ghost stories. A few years ago I published *Shapes That Haunt New England*, a collection of my fictional ghost stories.

   I soon found that, whenever I did book signings or gave readings or talks at libraries, people would tell me about ghosts they'd encountered, or haunted houses they'd lived in. Eventually I decided to follow up on the best of these, and as a result published *Haunters of the Dusk.* So it was fictional ghosts that led me to real ghosts.

2. **What do ghosts look like?** Ghosts seem to vary in the way they look. Some appear to be solid, and may at first be mistaken for actual people. Others may be clearly defined, yet transparent. Or they may be shadowy, or vaporous in appearance. And of course often they are not visible at all, but merely heard, or sensed.

165

3. **How do people contact ghosts?** Generally it is ghosts who initiate the contact. Of course, there are people who participate in seances in order to contact ghosts, but I have no expertise on that subject.

4. **Are there specific places where ghosts tend to haunt?** As for types of places, ghosts can haunt anywhere: old houses, new houses, automobiles, swamps, whatever. Some locales seem to lend themselves more than others to hauntings: perhaps where a violent crime was committed, or where someone suffered greatly (physically or emotionally).

5. **What is some of the gear researches use to find ghosts?** I can't help you on this one. Although I've spent many nights in haunted houses, hoping to encounter a ghost, I've never used any devices or equipment other than my senses.

6. **What is ghost dancing?** I'm not familiar with the term. [Perhaps the student was thinking of the Ghost Dance, a religious movement that began around 1850 with the western Indian tribes.]

7. **Can you explain what a poltergeist is?** A poltergeist is a ghost that makes noises or is otherwise disruptive (such as pelting houses or people with stones or other objects). Some have been known to repeatedly set fires, or cause objects to fly through the air, or to fall from walls or shelves, or to otherwise break. They are, I believe, never seen. Usually they are harmless, more a nuisance than otherwise. But occasionally they can be very hostile and dangerous.

8.   **Have you ever seen a ghost?** Unfortunately, no—despite my having spent the night in numerous haunted buildings. Some people seem to be far more sensitive than others in perceiving ghosts. Often, for whatever reason, those who most want to see a ghost seem to be the least likely to actually encounter one.

9.   **Do you know any way to contact ghosts?** No, other than to frequent places known to be haunted.

10. **What makes a ghost a ghost?** Or, what *is* a ghost? I don't know. Are they the spirits of dead people? Or some sort of psychic energy left over after a person dies? What about the ghosts of *living* persons, i.e., doppelgängers?

11. **What causes ghosts to appear?** Who knows? In some instances, it may be that the ghosts are always there, but are seen only by people who have a sort of sixth sense.

12. **What is the most interesting ghost story you have researched?** The hauntings on North Street, in Plymouth, Massachusetts—which I'm still researching—are rather interesting. You can read about some of them in *Ghosts in Black and White* [a copy of which I sent the student along with these answers—and the contents of which have been incorporated into this book].

13. **Do you have to go through any special training to become a ghost finder?** I really can't answer this one. I seek out ghost stories, rather than ghosts themselves.

Appendix Two

SPOOKS ON PARADE:
A Glossary of Ghostly Terms

The questions asked by the student in Maine (Appendix One) suggest that an annotated glossary defining the various types of ghosts a person is likely (or unlikely, depending on one's proclivities) to encounter might prove useful.

afreet (also spelled **afrit**): in Arabia, an evil spirit; the vengeful ghost of a murdered man, said to rise up from the spilled blood of the victim.

anniversary ghost: a ghost that appears or otherwise makes its presence known on a regular, usually yearly, basis, such as on the anniversary of the death of the person it "represents."

apparition: a ghostly figure or specter. In *The Encyclopedia of Ghosts and Spirits*, Rosemary Ellen Guiley gives a narrower definition— "the supernormal appearance of [a dead or living person or animal] too distant to be within the range of . . . normal perception." She further states that most "cases on record concern apparitions of the living and not of the dead"— and most are heard, felt, or otherwise sensed, rather than seen.

banshee (also spelled **banshie**): in Gaelic lore, a female spirit whose mournful wailing is heard before a death in the family. According to the editor of *Best Ghost Stories*, "The most famous Banshee of ancient times was that attached to the kingly house of O'Brien, Aibhill . . . In A.D. 1014 was fought the battle of Clontarf, from which the aged king, Brian Boru, knew that he would never come away alive, for the previous night Aibhill had appeared to him to tell him of

169

his impending fate."

bogy (also spelled **bogey** or **bogie**): an evil spirit; a hobgoblin. Not necessarily a ghost, but often mistaken for one. In her novella, *Cecilia de Noël*, Victorian author Lanoe Falconer (*nom de plume* of Mary Elizabeth Hawker) presents this exchange between two characters: "Not that she saw the ghost—not she. What she saw was a bogie, not a ghost." "Why, what is the difference?" "Immense! As big as that which separates the objective from the subjective. Anyone can see a bogie. It is a real thing belonging to the external world . . . always at night, you know, or at least in the dusk, when you are apt to be a little mixed in your observations."

doppelgänger: the ghostly double of a living person, the sighting of which often presages that person's death. The most effective use of the doppelgänger theme in fiction is in Edgar Allan Poe's classic short story, "William Wilson."

elemental: strictly speaking not an actual ghost, but a being of quite a different sort. E.F. Benson, in a classic short story, "And No Bird Sings," provides (through dialogue between two characters) an excellent description-cum-definition: "Was it a real material creature, or was it—" "Something ghostly, do you mean?" "Something halfway between the two." The two men are discussing something they've just encountered, "something like a huge phosphorescent slug." " . . . it is supposed to be some incarnation of evil. . . . not only spiritual [but] material to this extent—it can be seen, bodily in form, and heard, and . . . smelt, and God forbid, handled. It has to be kept alive by nourishment." Just what sort of nourishment can be learned by reading the above-mentioned story or Benson's equally classic, "Negotium Perambulans."

fetch: a ghostly double of a living person, i.e., doppelgänger.

hant (i.e., **haunt**): Southern dialectal term for *ghost*.

poltergeist: (defined in Appendix One, Question Seven.) Perhaps the most notorious example of a poltergeist, at least in America, is the so-called Bell Witch, about which numerous articles and books have been written. Susy Smith in *Prominent American Ghosts* and Daniel Cohen in *The Encyclopedia of Ghosts* both provide succinct accounts of this prolonged haunting that began in 1817 in Tennessee.

radiant boy: the apparition of a young boy, glowing with a bright light or surrounded by flame. There are two beliefs concerning the origin of radiant boys: the first, that they are beings from the world of spirits who have recently taken on human form; the second (and more common belief), that they are the ghosts of children murdered by their mothers. In either case, they are omens of bad luck or sudden death.

revenant: one who returns after death; a ghost.

screaming skull: many instances of skulls which scream or otherwise cause disturbances have been cited. Generally, the skulls become active when they are moved from a particular building, vault, or other location. Elliott O'Donnell recounts the legend of "The Screaming Skulls of Calgarth Hall" in *The Screaming Skulls and Other Ghosts*. In *Ghosts Over England*, R. Thurston Hopkins devotes an entire chapter to a number of troublesome skulls. He begins "Skullduggery" with this statement: "There are told of certain houses . . . many weird skull stories, the popular idea being that if an impious hand should be foolish enough to move . . . such grisly relics, death and misfortune will inevitably overtake some member of the family." The best (in my estimation) fictional treatment of the theme is F. Marion Crawford's "The Screaming Skull," available in any number of anthologies.

shade: a ghost, especially one dwelling in the underworld.

shape: an imaginary or ghostly form; a phantom (as in *Shapes That Haunt New England*, my first collection of ghost stories).

specter: a ghost, especially one that is seen.

spook: a ghost.

wraith: the apparition of a living person (see *fetch* and *doppelgänger*); the ghost of a dead person.

SOURCES AND BOOKS MENTIONED IN THE TEXT

Along New England Shores by A. Hyatt Verrill (New York: G.P. Putnam's Sons, 1936).

Among the Isles of Shoals by Celia Thaxter (Boston: James R. Osgood and Company, 1873).

The Best Ghost Stories, ed. by Arthur B. Reeve (New York: Carlton House, n.d.).

A Book of New England Legends and Folk Lore by Samuel Adams Drake (Boston: Roberts Brothers, 1884).

The Collected Ghost Stories of E.F. Benson, ed. by Richard Dalby (New York: Carroll & Graf Publishers, Inc., 1996).

Colonial Architecture of Cape Cod, Nantucket, and Martha's Vineyard by Alfred Easton Poor (New York: William Helburn, Inc., 1932. Reprinted by Dover Publications, Inc., 1970).

Elegant Nightmares: The English Ghost Story from Le Fanu to Blackwood by Jack Sullivan (Athens, Ohio: Athens University Press, 1978).

The Encyclopedia of Ghosts by Daniel Cohen (New York: Dorset Press, 1989).

The Encyclopedia of Ghosts and Spirits by Rosemary Ellen Guiley (New York: Facts On File, Inc., 1992).

The Ghost Stories of Edith Wharton (New York: Charles Scribner's Sons, 1973).

Ghosts in Black and White: Some Hauntings in Plymouth County (a chapbook) by Edward Lodi (Middleborough, Massachusetts: Rock Village Publishing, 2001).

Ghosts Over England by R. Thurston Hopkins (London: Meridian Books, 1953).

Haunters of the Dusk by Edward Lodi (Middleborough, Massachusetts: Rock Village Publishing, 2001).

Historic Hallowell, compiled by Katherine H. Snell and Vincent P. Ledew. (Designed and Printed by The Kennebec Journal Print Shop, 1962).

An Island Garden by Celia Thaxter (1894; facsimile edition 2002 by Houghton Mifflin).

Jonathan Draws the Long Bow by Richard M. Dorson (Cambridge, Massachusetts: Harvard University Press, 1946).

Legends and Otherwise of Hallowell and Loudon Hill by Edward Preble Norton (Augusta, Maine: The Press of Charles E. Nash & Son, 1923).

Maine Ghosts and Legends: 26 Encounters with the Supernatural by Thomas A. Verde (Camden, Maine: Down East Books, 1989).

Memories of North Carver Village by Ellsworth C. Braddock (Marion, Massachusetts: Channing Books, 1977).

The Mammoth Book of Haunted House Stories edited by Peter Haining (New York: Carroll & Graf Publishers, Inc., 2000).

Myths & Legends of Our Own Land (in two volumes) by Charles M. Skinner (Philadelphia: J.B. Lippincott Company, 1896).

New England: Indian Summer 1865-1915 by Van Wyck Brooks (E.P. Dutton & Co., Inc. 1940).

The Old Colony Town and the Ambit of Buzzards Bay by William Root Bliss (Boston: Houghton, Mifflin and Company, 1893).

Old Plymouth Trails by Winthrop Packard (Boston: Small, Maynard & Company, 1920).

Passport to the Supernatural by Bernhardt J. Hurwood (New York: Taplinger Publishing Company, 1972).

Plymouth Memories of an Octogenarian by William T. Davis (Plymouth, Massachusetts: Memorial Press, 1906).

Prominent American Ghosts by Susy Smith (Cleveland and New York: The World Publishing Company, 1967).

The Ropemakers of Plymouth: A History of the Plymouth Cordage Company 1824-1949 by Samuel Eliot Morison (Boston: Houghton Mifflin Company, 1950).

The Screaming Skulls and Other Ghosts by Elliott O'Donnell (New York: Taplinger Publishing Co., Inc., 1969).

September Days on Nantucket by William Root Bliss (Boston: Houghton, Mifflin and Company, 1902).

Shadows and Cypress: Southern Ghost Stories compiled by Alan Brown (Jackson, Mississippi: University of Mississippi Press, 2000).

Sleep No More ed. by August Derleth (New York: Farrar & Rinehart, Inc., 1944).

True Tales of the Weird by Sidney Dickinson (New York: Duffield and Company, 1920).

Victorian Ghost Stories by Noted Women Writers, ed. by Richard Dalby (New York: Barnes & Noble, 1996).

What They Say in New England: A Book of Signs, Sayings, and Superstitions collected by Clifton Johnson (Boston: Lee and Shepard Publishers, 1896).

177